Praise for the works of Riley Scott

A Time to Speak

This book is a romance, murder mystery, political statement, and family drama all rolled into one, and it pulls off all facets in fine style. Amelia is in the closet, so far back in it she could see Narnia. Dominique is a great blend of strong with a hint of vulnerable. Alongside the two leading women, Scott has also created portrayals of some key figures in the town. When I first started reading these multiple points of view I feared I'd get lost in all their stories, or that it would be spread a bit thin. Groundless fears, it turns out, as Scott's masterful use of these points of view only adds delicious richness to the story. It is fantastic writing, brilliant weaving of a story, and I couldn't put it down. Highly recommended.

-Rainbow Book Reviews

I really liked the tone of the book. It would be too easy to have created a dark story of inner turmoil and grief, with negative emotions and a violent display of ignorance and discrimination. Riley Scott, however, tells the story with almost a confidence that, even if it is only possible to win the fight with one person, then that one person is important.

Backstage

Backstage Pass is a celebrity romance with an out-of-control rock goddess and her new PR rep. It's a little grittier than I'm used to seeing in celebrity romances, and it works well. Reading a new-to-me author is always an adventure because I never know if I'm going to like them, love them, or walk away and never look back. I had never read anything by Riley Scott before, and I was more than pleasantly surprised by how much I enjoyed this book. It's very well plotted and perfectly paced, and I found myself wanting to shut out the world so I could just focus on *Backstage Pass*.

-The Lesbian Review

This is a great read. Strong personalities, a solid and well-drawn setting and a plausible and well-constructed plot. Riley Scott fills in detail on a wide range of characters as well as Raven and Chris, creating a good grounding for the plausibility of their interactions. Their behaviours are believable, and even when Chris breaks her own rules we can see how she has been swept up in the rush of life on the road.

-Lesbian Reading Room

Take Your Shot

Other Bella Books by Riley Scott

Backstage Pass
Conservative Affairs
On the Rocks
Small Town Secrets
A Time to Speak

About the Author

In addition to having published poetry and short stories, Riley Scott has worked as a grant and press writer and a marketing professional. She holds a degree in journalism. Riley's love for fiction began at a young age, and she has been penning stories for over a decade. Her days and her writing alike are fueled by strong coffee, humor, people watching, and just enough daydreaming to craft imaginative novels. She lives in Pensacola, Florida, with the love of her life and their three beloved dogs, as well as six chickens who provide comic relief, as well as breakfast.

Take Your Shot

Riley Scott

BELLA
BOOKS
2022

Printed in the United States of America on acid-free paper.

First Edition - 2022

Editor: Kay Grey
Cover Artwork: Heather Dickerman
Cover Designer: Judith Fellows

ISBN: 978-1-64247-353-7

PUBLISHER'S NOTE

Acknowledgment

Bringing to life any story takes a fair amount of time, research, and support. I'm beyond grateful to my wife, who indulges me by listening to me chatter on endlessly about characters she hasn't yet met, listening to music that I think just *fits* the story, brainstorming ideas with me, and of course taking over the cooking while I hole up in my office and write. This story was inspired by my wife, who asked me one day years ago if we would have dated in high school. We laughed and dreamt up a scenario, where I was on the basketball team, and she was a reporter for the school newspaper. While that was only the starting point for two characters who took on lives, personalities, and stories of their own, I credit her for being such a strong influence on my creativity and my belief in love that conquers all. Thank you, my love, for your unwavering support and for lending your artistic talents to create such a fun book cover.

As a former basketball player and lifelong lover of the game, it was a pleasure to revisit my glory days and breathe life into this story. I'm grateful to my teammates for the lasting memories, and to my former hometown of Albuquerque, New Mexico, for the many wonderful experiences I had there. It was an incredible experience to relive moments, both on the court and at my old stomping grounds, through this story.

I'm incredibly grateful for Kay Grey, who helped me edit this story and bring it to life. Thank you to my friends in the Twitter community for always providing support and encouragement when I need it the most. Thank you to the readers who encourage me and continue to devour books, so we can all write more. Thank you to one of my old friends and an amazing math teacher for walking me through a calculus lesson via text, but making sure I didn't actually have to learn it, since

I'm mathematically challenged. Also, thank you to every one of my friends who answers my random texts for book research purposes, whether it's playlist inspiration, quotes, or fashion. Finally, I am eternally grateful to my friends and family who keep me laughing each day, support my work, and remind me of all the beauty in the world.

Dedication

For all who have struggled to find their own identity, all the queer youth waiting for the right time to come out, all who have had to face insurmountable trauma and come out stronger on the other side, all the basketball fans, budding journalists, music lovers, and dreamers, this story was written with you in mind.

Logan's Playlist for Carter

Listen on Spotify – "Take Your Shot" by Riley Scott
The Beatles – "I Want to Hold Your Hand"
Dua Lipa – "If It Ain't Me"
Halsey – "Finally // beautiful stranger"
Ruth B. – "Dandelions"
Joan Jett & The Blackhearts – "Crimson and Clover"
Adaline – "Cross the Line"
blink-182 – "All the Small Things"
Gia Woods – "Only a Girl"
Faime – "Feels Like You"

CHAPTER ONE

Around her, sneakers squeaked on the cheap tile of the school hallway. The fluorescent bulbs overhead whirred, and in the distance, Carter could hear the click of someone's heels.

Who was impractical enough to wear heels to high school? She shook her head, drowning out the noise of the hundreds of voices, and focused on the book in her hand.

"Could you be any more predictable?" Her best friend, Aiden, leaned against the locker next to her, smiling. He was always far more chipper than should have been allowed before eight o'clock in the morning.

"I don't know what you're talking about." She shrugged, marked her place in the book with a receipt from this morning's coffee purchase and shoved it in her locker.

"Let's see." Aiden laughed and held up his hand to count off his list dramatically. "Number one, we've got the oversized iced coffee, despite the snow on the ground outside. Number two, we're reading Poe this morning. How very on-brand and gloomy for you. And, number three, what *is* that lip color?"

Carter brought her hand up to her mouth, defensively touching her lips. "What's wrong with it?"

"It's amazing," he said, shaking his head. "It's not an insult… It's just…it's purple."

"I thought I'd try out something new." She pushed her glasses up on her nose and looked him up and down. "You're one to talk about predictability," she said, shaking her head. "You look like you're ready for a job interview at a CPA firm."

"Is the bow tie too much?" He adjusted it and ran a hand through his shoulder-length blond hair.

"Probably, considering we're only on our way to AP English."

"Here," he said, handing her a breakfast burrito. "This is to keep the peace after interrupting your reading."

"Thank you," she said, taking it and inspecting the yellow wrapper from her favorite breakfast joint. She held the warm gift in her hand and breathed it in, smiling as she saw the writing on the side of the wrapper. "Egg, cheese, potato, and green chile?"

"Would I get you anything else?"

She thought about hugging him, but offered a smile instead. As she unwrapped the bundle of joy—a true gift from the gods if there ever were one—she glanced across the hallway and watched as the doors from the gym opened.

Freshly showered, and somehow miraculously put together, the basketball team breezed into the school building as if they were on a runway. She could picture it—a fog machine, dance music playing, and each of them taking their chance to walk down the hallway and do a turn. She shook her head. Even without the added theatrics, it was quite the show. Morning practices were another gift from the gods, she decided. She tried to swallow a bite of her burrito and choked, as her mouth went dry.

Was it considered gay panic if she wasn't afraid of her sexuality, but was just a lesbian who had anxiety around every pretty girl she saw? She pondered the thought, as she forced herself to look away from the beauty before her. Of course, there were a couple of them who stood out, but all of them had the power to turn her into an even bigger sports fan than she already was.

"You show every emotion on your face." Aiden's laughter beside her drew her out of her thoughts. "Why don't you try talking to one of them one day?"

She shook her head, quickly dismissing the notion.

"Oh, is there one in particular?"

"No," she snapped. "There's not. And there probably won't be. Not here anyway." She sighed and looked at the calendar in her locker. "Not until next year."

"Why not?"

She stared at him, trying to figure out if it was ignorance or just his lack of dating that made him ask the question. Perhaps it was a little of both.

"In order to have a relationship between two girls, both parties involved have to, in fact, like girls." She exhaled sharply and took another bite of her burrito.

"You're going to sit there and tell me that not one single female basketball player at this school bats for your team?"

"Oh, come on, I know you know that's the wrong sport," she shot back, looking back to where the crowd of players had now dispersed.

Directly across from her, she watched as Logan Watts chatted with her boyfriend, Barrett. She heard Logan's laugh ring out into the stuffy air, changing the atmosphere for a second and adding an ethereal element. Logan smiled and turned away from him, pulling her thick, long hair into a ponytail. Its color was like amber honey, somewhere between blond and brunette, and adding yet another layer to Logan's beauty. As she reached up to secure her hair, the movement pulled her hoodie up just above the top of her jeans, exposing the small of her back.

Carter looked away, not wanting to exploit the moment.

"What is wrong with you?" Aiden asked, stepping between her and Logan.

"Nothing." She finished her burrito and walked past Aiden, tossing the wrapper in the trash. "Thank you for breakfast. I've got you covered tomorrow."

"Deal." He grabbed his books and fell in step beside her, as they followed Logan and Barrett toward the English room.

Barrett grabbed Logan's hand, and Carter winced.

"Are you jealous?"

"No," she said. "I mean, not of him." She kept her voice low, her eyes never leaving their entwined hands. "I just don't think they have any idea how lucky they are."

"Those two?" Aiden stopped and turned to face Carter. "They're in a sham of a relationship if I've ever seen one."

"They look pretty happy to me," she said, craning her neck to watch them for another second as they turned around the corner.

"Word on the street is they don't even sleep together."

Carter laughed at the grimace on Aiden's face. "You know, first of all, that's none of our business. Second, you don't have to have sex with someone just to be in a relationship."

"True." He popped a piece of gum in his mouth and nodded, as if he was considering the fact. "But, I guess her logic is that she doesn't want to get pregnant and screw up her scholarship to UNM." He shifted his weight and his stack of books to gesture with his right hand. Holding his hand in the air, he wagged his finger. "Everyone knows there's birth control."

"She doesn't owe anyone an explanation, not even Barrett. If you're trying to make me feel better, this weird anti-feminist shit isn't the way to do it."

"Sorry." He glanced down to the floor. "I guess you're right. Just seems like there's something missing there."

"There might be, but as two people who have virtually zero dating experience, I don't think we get a say."

"Fine." He resumed the walk to class and put his arm around her. "But, I'd like the record to show I called it when they don't last."

"Noted."

As she took her seat, she fought to keep her eyes off Logan. Was it lust or a crush, or was she just enamored by someone who looked so confident, so at ease with herself? Liking girls was confusing sometimes. She bit her lip, as she watched Logan fish something out of her backpack and then lean back in her chair.

The level of coolness, without all the usual jackassery that came with it, just seemed impossible somehow. Logan stretched her neck side to side and glanced over in Carter's direction. She smiled and nodded, before turning her eyes to the front of the room. Carter's breath caught in her throat. She dropped her pencil to the desk, grabbing it quickly before it rolled to the ground. She gulped and looked down at the floor to still her thoughts. She'd been caught staring like a creep.

She grabbed the Hydro Flask from her bag and took a long sip, hoping her heart rate would return to normal at some point.

CHAPTER TWO

Mr. Garcia droned on about calculus in front of the classroom, and Logan was sure her eyes were going to glaze over. No matter how many times he explained it, none of it made sense. Sure, she could memorize formulas and plug in numbers better than most, but what did it even mean?

She felt a sharp sting in her right shoulder and winced. Rotating it slightly, she bit her lip to quell the pain. She glanced around, making sure no one noticed. The last thing she needed was for word to get back to coach that she was still hurting. She'd managed to pull it off well enough for the past week and wasn't going to let a lingering injury keep her from continuing into the most important year of her career. Still, she felt like she was a thirty-something, always being overly careful of how she moved or slept so she wasn't in pain.

Leaning back in her chair, she resisted the urge to pull the hood of her sweatshirt up over her head and lay down on the desk. The early morning practices, combined with evening practice, homework, and trying to have a life outside of it all had taken their toll. She looked around the room, wondering if anyone else understood this more than she did. Glancing over her shoulder, one seat back and to the right, she saw the girl who had been staring at her this morning. Carter Shaw, editor of the *Albuquerque Prep Gazette*. They were in three honors classes together, and Logan had seen her around throughout the years. She was sure there was more to the girl, but she was best known for her school newspaper and for being one of the smartest students in the school.

They'd never spoken, but Logan was sure if anyone understood calculus, Carter did. She always had her head in a book and seemed to ace every test she ever took without a struggle. Logan smiled, thinking of how Carter's weekly column in the school paper always held some sort of wisdom, a deep message, or even just musical suggestions. She watched Carter as she scribbled on the page in front of her.

Was she taking notes? Was there something noteworthy happening, or was she drawing because she was as bored as everyone else in the class? Logan wanted to lean back to get a closer view, but knew doing so would catch the attention of Mr. Garcia. The last thing she needed was to get busted for not paying attention—again. She stifled a sigh. What was the point of paying attention if she still got As?

She's definitely drawing, Logan decided. Amused, she watched the furious scribble of Carter's pencil. Her long fingers were smudged with pencil markings all the way to her fingernails that were painted with black matte polish. Somehow, Carter had gotten past the fashion police enforcers that usually patrolled the halls, making sure no one wore hats or baggy pants, and she was proudly and adorably rocking a dark beanie. It was like the cherry on top of a sundae, the way it paired with her plaid flannel and high-waisted jeans. Logan's smile grew, as she thanked the powers that be that their school board had voted to abolish school uniforms.

If nothing else, it gave her a chance to observe the world of fashion through others. She looked down at her favorite red hoodie, with her number, eleven, emblazoned on a basketball in the middle and her last name across the back. Maybe she'd try to dress in a trendy fashion one day.

"Miss Watts, what do you think?" Mr. Garcia's voice boomed.

Her cheeks grew hot, as heads around her turned in her direction. Carter's gaze was first, locking eyes with her for the second time of the day. She dropped her eyes to the ground and then stared at the board covered in letters and formulas. She racked her brain. They'd been going over the Mean Value Theorem all morning, and she could recite the formula and even solve the problem on the board, but truthfully she had no idea of what he'd even asked.

She'd been so deep into admiring Carter's outfit that she'd spaced out the last half hour. She cleared her throat.

"I don't know," she admitted, leaning back in her chair.

She heard giggles in the back of the room, but knew they weren't directed at her. For some reason, a handful of her classmates always thought it was cool to blow off everything the teacher said with nonchalance, so by her dumbing it down, she'd just earned more 'cool points.' She gulped, detesting the cool points, even as she was thankful for the fact she wasn't the laughing stock.

"Let's focus our eyes up here then," Mr. Garcia said. He gave her a tight-lipped grin and tapped his marker on the white board.

She nodded and hoped the blush on her cheeks wasn't noticeable. Out of the corner of her eye, she saw Carter stare at her curiously, while rolling her pencil through her fingers, as if trying to solve the puzzle. Only this time, it wasn't the Mean Value Theorem. It was Logan. She straightened in her chair and leaned forward, doing her best to at least feign interest in the subject at hand.

Her phone buzzed in her pocket. She furrowed her brow. The last thing she needed was another thing vying for her attention, but she let curiosity win. She glanced at the screen. It was a text from her best friend, Josie.

What's going on with you?

She looked over her left shoulder, where Josie raised an eyebrow in her direction.

She gave a thumbs-up sign and turned back around. Her phone buzzed again, but this time she ignored it. By the time the bell rang, she bolted for the door.

She needed to focus on getting through her next class. She glanced at her phone to check the time and made a beeline for her locker to switch books. As she rounded the corner to the row of lockers, she stopped in her tracks. Barrett was already waiting for her, and he was pacing in front of her locker.

"What's up?" She looked him up and down. When he said nothing, she stepped around him and switched out the book in her hand for her chemistry book.

"Why am I getting texts that you were drooling all over the smarty spice lesbian during calculus—so much so that you couldn't answer a single question?"

"Lesbian?" Logan crinkled her forehead. "What?" As soon as the words were out of her mouth, she gasped. Her mouth went dry, and she shoved her hands in her pockets. She opened her mouth to speak, but her thoughts ran rampant. Carter was a lesbian, so everyone clearly thought *that's* why she was staring. "No," she said, looking down to the ground and then around her. Even though no one was looking at her, she felt like all eyes were on her. "I wasn't."

"What's going on then? Two of the guys were texting me about how you couldn't seem to tear your eyes away, and you had this goofy, lovestruck smile the whole time."

"I didn't." Logan shook her head. "I like her beanie. I want one."

He eyed her carefully, then shrugged.

Logan cleared her throat and grabbed Barrett's hand. "Hey, why are you jealous of her? I'm with you."

"It's just what a couple of the guys in class said." He tightened his grip on her hand. "I don't know. I just wanted to check with you before anyone else said anything."

"News sure travels fast around here." She shook her head. "It was nothing. It started out because she was drawing something, and I wanted to see what it was. Then, I was thinking about how warm her beanie must be. I think I was half daydreaming to be completely honest. I need to start getting more sleep."

The words tumbled out quickly, as she covered her tracks, but it did nothing to slow her erratic heartbeat. What had she been doing? She'd spent half an hour doing exactly what they said— drooling over the cute lesbian girl in class. It didn't matter that Carter was fashionable or cute. She shouldn't even be thinking that way. She was straight. She had a boyfriend, after all.

Barrett was talking, but she wasn't listening. As they parted ways, he leaned in and kissed her, taking her lips in his possessively. She stiffened, but accepted the kiss. He headed off toward his shop class, and she turned on a heel. She laughed at the thought that a man as seemingly tough as the captain of the state championship-winning football team, who she'd dated for three years, could be insecure about the fact that she was admiring another girl's clothing. She shook her head and made her way to the chemistry classroom.

At least Carter wasn't in this class, and only a couple of quiet kids from the calculus class were here. She needed an escape somehow, and more than anything, she needed to get her head in the game. It was no secret she'd been off recently. That's how her parents explained it.

I know you're still getting good grades, and you're killin' it on the court. Something is just off.

She could hear her mom's voice in the back of her head, but she took a deep breath, exhaling and pushing the thoughts away. There would be time to sort that all out one day, or maybe she wouldn't even need to. She was young. She was resilient. She'd figure it all out. In the meantime, no one would be the wiser.

Taking her seat, she pulled her book from her backpack and flipped to the chapter they'd been studying. Busying herself, she kept her eyes on the pages in front of her. She read in a hurry, and the words blurred. She retained nothing, but to the naked eye, maybe she'd just look like a dutiful student. Maybe she could disguise her panicked inner monologue. She swallowed hard and forced herself to breathe normally.

Who cares what anyone thinks, anyway?

Her racing heart gave her the answer to her question. Clearly, *she* cared. But she ignored it, looking straight ahead, as if once more needing the help of the periodic table in the front of the room, even though she'd long since memorized it. She straightened her posture, only to wince again at the stinging pain in her shoulder.

Cursing under her breath, she resumed her comfortable slouch. It would seem weird if she presented differently today, she decided. She was overthinking things, but then again, she had a habit of doing that.

As Mrs. Washington called the class to order, stepping to the front, draped in a bright yellow dress that could really only be pulled off by someone who deemed herself a mad scientist in jest, Logan took a deep breath.

Her normal morning routine had quickly devolved into a state of panic, but it didn't have to continue in that fashion. Everyone would soon forget about her staring at Carter, and they'd have some other anecdote to share about their own classes.

She glanced to the whiteboard, where Mrs. Washington was presenting, and sighed with relief as her body found its way out of its panic response. Opening her notebook, she jotted notes, stopping halfway through her sentence to look at the board and try to comprehend what was being said.

For once, she understood the jokes about Charlie Brown's teacher in the old cartoons her grandma used to play for her and her brothers when they'd visit. She smiled at the memory, and leaned back in her chair.

* * *

"Logan." Mrs. Washington's voice was soft and kind, drawing Logan from her dream. *Mrs. Washington!* Logan's eyes flew open, and she jerked her body back, staring up at Mrs. Washington's bemused expression. "Class is over."

Logan's eyes darted around the room. She was the only one remaining. How embarrassing! Had she snored? How long had she been out? She tried to remember, but couldn't recall anything past the first five minutes of class.

"I'm so sorry," she said, grabbing her things, and stepping from her desk.

"You've been taking on a lot for a student." Mrs. Washington's words were slow, as if she was choosing each word carefully. "You're not in trouble with me, but I do have to send you to the counselor's office. I've noticed you trailing off a lot lately, and I want to make sure you're okay."

Logan grimaced. She nodded and shoved her books into her bag. It could be worse. She could have dozed off in Mr. Garcia's class. She knew he would have shown no mercy. "Thank you. I mean, thanks for not sending me to Rumble's office." She shuddered, thinking of their intolerable principal.

"That's Dr. Rumble to you." Mrs. Washington's laugh echoed through the room, but not before she put her hand on her hip. "I think you need to go to the counselor's office on your lunch break today. I don't want you to miss out on any of your other classes, but this is important."

"Do I have to skip lunch?"

"You can grab something quick and then go before your afternoon classes." Her tone was gentle but nonnegotiable.

Logan wanted to protest, but knew it would do her no good. The woman was a saint of a teacher, every bit as eccentric as she was brilliant and nurturing, but even she had her limits. As a straight-A student-athlete, Logan knew better than to cross her allies.

Her final classes of the morning passed without incident, thankfully, but she couldn't clear her mind of her impending meeting with the counselor. She'd talked about her feelings enough over the past two years, and she hadn't made any progress in "healing," or "getting over it," whatever that even meant. After fourth period, she headed to her locker to store her books.

In front of her locker, Barrett was waiting for her. He was like a lost puppy, always waiting for her to make his next move. He greeted her with a kiss, pulling her tight against him. "Not now," she mumbled, pushing him away. "I have to go to the counselor's office."

"But we have plans," he protested. For a legal adult, he sure pouted a lot.

"*You* have plans," she corrected. "I have to go."

"I'm taking you for burgers, remember?"

"That has to wait. Like I said, I can't get out of it. Not today." She forced herself past him, dumped her books, and walked away before he could ask any more questions. The last thing she wanted to do right now was face yet another interrogation.

She'd grab a protein bar from her gym bag on her way to fifth period, but for now, she just wanted to get this over with. She was tired of talking to people who outwardly seemed like they had good intentions, but really just wanted to know what was wrong with her.

She wanted to scream. They should all know what was wrong. Part of her died two years ago, and life was never going to go back to *normal*, if normal even existed. Sure, she could keep playing ball, going to school, and focusing on the future, but that didn't change the past. Nothing could.

Holding her head high, she knocked on the semiopen door with the emblazoned "Counselor" plate.

"Come in," Susan called out in a singsong. Susan, who insisted the students call her by her first name in some kind of ruse to get them to trust her more, was always a bit too bright and sunny for Logan's liking. "Ah, Miss Watts." She smiled and motioned for Logan to step inside. "What can I do for you today?"

"I…I, uh, fell asleep in chemistry today, and Mrs. Washington sent me over to talk to you."

"Wouldn't that normally be an offense handled by Dr. Rumble, instead of me?"

"On any normal day, maybe, but she had mercy on my soul."

Susan laughed, and then looked immediately down, as if she didn't know how to handle dry wit. "Well then, I suppose let's chat about what led up to you falling asleep in class?" Susan crinkled her brow and flipped through her files until she pulled a folder with Logan's name on it. She quickly scanned the contents, while Logan waited. After a moment, she settled back into her chair and made eye contact again.

"I'm not really sure." Logan looked behind Susan to the picture of cats clad in matching knitted sweaters. Even though she was sure they had it worse than she did, she would have gladly traded places with those cats for the afternoon, just to get out of the hot seat.

"Stress at home? At school?"

Everywhere, Logan thought, but instead offered a smile. "No, not really. Things are fine. I think these early morning practices just got the best of me."

"Susan, have you seen my..." Dr. Rumble's loud voice from the adjoining office came to a halt, as he opened the door and saw Logan sitting there. "Excuse me," he said in Logan's direction. "I thought all students would be at lunch right now."

"So did I," Logan mumbled under her breath.

"What did you say?" His deep voice always came across so condescending and grating.

Logan cleared her throat. "Nothing. I was just talking with Susan about..." She trailed off, wondering how to fill the gap without getting busted by the big man in charge.

"Hmm, I see," he said, when she refused to fill in the sentence. "Well, get back to it. Susan, when you're done, let me know if you see my stapler."

He turned to leave, and Susan turned her attention back to Logan. "Falling asleep in class isn't a huge deal," she started, but Logan glanced up, realizing Dr. Rumble was still in the process of shutting the door.

"Falling asleep in class, huh?" he asked, turning back to face her. "You know we have a student handbook that states that students who sleep through, skip, or otherwise miss a class must make it up?"

For the millionth time, she wished she could have gone to public school like the rest of the world. Sure, opportunities were great and all, but did it have to be run like such a dictatorship? There was no room for human error or human behavior like falling asleep around here, it seemed. She straightened in her chair and offered him a polite smile. "I apologize, sir. I fell asleep for a few minutes. Just had a really early morning with practice." Knowing he was a sports fan, she was hoping to appease his better side, but his tight-lipped expression told her she wasn't winning this one. "How can I make it up?"

"After school study hall on Thursday."

"We have a game on Thursday," she said, her mind racing through the possibilities. She couldn't miss the first district game of her senior year. "It's out of town. We're leaving right after sixth period."

He shook his head. "Sorry, Logan. You should have thought about that before you blew off class."

"Can I make it up *any* other day?"

"Thursday."

"Okay," she said, holding up her hands to plead her case. "How will I get to the game if I can't go on the bus?"

"Can't you drive?" The sentence was out of his mouth before he could stop it, and Logan saw the regret on his face after it was spoken. "Right," he said quietly. "Well, maybe you can ride with your parents."

"They're not going to be able to make it Thursday. Dad has a court case, and Mom is out of town."

"Catch a ride with a friend or something." He shoved his hands into his pockets. She stifled a sigh. He knew how important this was to her, but his track record of yielding or leading with leniency wasn't stellar.

"By the time any of them finish up with their own practices, they'll get to the game right at tip-off. That's not an option. I have to be there earlier."

"Hmmm…I know," he said, walking briefly into his office. He returned with a slip of paper. "You can go with…um…hold on a minute." He scanned the paper in his hands. "Right here," he said, pointing to a name. "Carter Shaw. She just turned in this slip from the newspaper. Looks like she's leaving right around the time you'd need to head out of here to get over to Gallup to cover the game for the paper."

Logan's mouth went dry. Why was everything about Carter today?

"Maybe Ben can take me." Her little brother was her last hope.

"He'll be in practice, as well, Logan." Dr. Rumble's tone was so patronizing, she wasn't even a bit sorry for all the times kids walked by his office singing the cheesy old warm-up song, "Let's Get Ready to Rumble." She sighed.

"Carter it is." She said, forcing a smile until he walked out.

"Well," Logan said, looking to Susan when the door finally shut. "Are we done here, since I've already received my punishment?"

"I'm so sorry," Susan said. Her eyes looked like she wanted to say more, but Logan tossed her hands in the air, trying to downplay the frustration she felt.

"No harm, no foul. It's fine. I'll still make the game. Now, can I go grab lunch?"

"Sure." Susan nodded. "Just try to take care of yourself and get a good night's sleep a little more often."

Logan nodded, grabbing her things and heading back to her locker. The way this school and its leadership handled problems was nothing short of absurd, she thought.

As she bit into her protein bar, she had to laugh at the sheer irony of this day from hell. Somehow, Carter Shaw was going to be her stylish knight in shining armor, after all.

CHAPTER THREE

Thankful for a minute of peace and quiet that seemed such a far cry from the normal bustling of over-stimulated high schoolers, Carter took a second to ground herself and focus on her breathing. Even though she was one of their peers, something about the hype and drama tossed about so easily by the others just made her feel like she didn't belong here. It was a strange sanctuary, but the bathroom nearest the senior lockers was all but abandoned during the lunch hour, making it one of her chosen hideouts.

Staring at her reflection in the mirror, she adjusted her forest green beanie. How she'd made it the whole day without being asked to take it off was beyond her, but it was a gamble that paid off. She had to admit, she liked it, even if she was skeptical when Aiden talked her into buying it at the mall the weekend before.

It seemed like she wasn't the only one either, judging by the way Logan Watts had been staring at her in calculus. She wiped the silly grin off her face, and forced a neutral expression. It meant nothing. The girl was straight. She had a boyfriend.

But it still didn't hurt Carter's confidence to have drawn her attention—regardless of the reason.

She heard the door creak open. *So much for a minute of alone time.* Turning to leave, she came face-to-face with Logan.

"Oh hey!" Logan said.

Carter took a step back and tilted her head to the side. This was new. Not that their paths hadn't crossed. They just didn't usually speak.

"Hey," Carter said. She wanted to say something clever, but nothing came to mind.

"I was actually hoping to chat with you before the end of the day." Logan leaned against the tile wall.

"You were?"

"Yeah." Logan flashed her a bright smile. Carter's heart pounded. She shoved her hands in her pockets, trying to maintain even breathing. "Seems like Dr. Rumble volunteered you to help me out."

"Me?" Carter's eyes widened in confusion. "With what?"

"You're going to the game Thursday, right?"

"Yeah, what's the deal? You need me to help wrap your ankle or something?" Carter laughed nervously. Why would she say that? And, even more, why would she admit that she'd observed enough to know that Logan always wrapped her ankle before the game.

To her relief, Logan laughed. "No, I think Coach Newcomb has that part covered." She bit her lip, for the first time Carter had seen, looking unsure. She crossed her arms over her chest. "I got in a little trouble in chemistry and have to do a makeup period after class, so I'll miss the bus."

"Oh no, that sucks."

"Yeah"—Logan nodded—"it really does. But, I guess since you're going, and no one else is around who will also be there in time for warm-ups and stuff, Dr. Rumble said I needed to ride with you."

"Oh!" Carter's voice was too high. She cleared her throat.

"Is that okay?"

Carter looked into Logan's blue eyes and nodded, unable to form words. Logan's smile grew.

"Cool, thank you." She laughed, and Carter couldn't tell what was funny, but she laughed too. "Sorry about it. I'll try to be a good travel buddy."

"Yeah, you'll be the best." Carter glanced down at her feet. She needed to get it together before Thursday, if they were going to be in a car together for two hours. "Go, Cougars," she said, awkwardly nodding as she made her way toward the door. If Logan hadn't been in sight, she would have buried her head in her hands.

"Oh, wait," Logan called after her. "Do you want my number?"

"Uh." Carter stared at her, searching for words.

"You know, for Thursday, so we know where and when to meet up?"

"Oh right, yeah…sure." She fished her phone out of her pocket and handed it over to Logan, who typed her number onto the screen.

"There you go," Logan said, smiling as she handed the phone back. As their fingers brushed, Carter pulled her hand away quickly.

"I'll text you here in a few, so you have my number too."

"Great! Thanks again."

"Yeah, anytime." As she turned to leave this time, she hoped to whatever powers may be that she wasn't blushing. She saved the number and shoved her phone in her pocket. She took a couple of steps and then pulled it out. She'd said she'd text Logan. She stared at the screen, before putting it back in her pocket. She'd do that later, after she'd had a chance to figure out what to say. It should be simple, right? Just send a "hey" or maybe a "hi." She glanced at her watch and was thankful to see lunchtime was wrapping up.

Unlike some of the others, she didn't see the point in prolonging breaks from classes. The sooner she could get into class, the sooner she could get out, and eventually she'd graduate and be on to bigger and better things at college.

College. The word flashed in her head like a neon sign, and with it the looming decisions that had to be made. There was the safety net of an academic scholarship and the comforts of home down the road at the University of New Mexico, or there was the unknown of New York City—a place she'd dreamt and written about since she was a child, but had never so much as visited. Was it a pipe dream, something that seemed better in her head than it would be in reality, or was it something she really wanted?

Thankful to retreat into the privacy of the newspaper office—a room that had served as nothing more than an oversized closet for copier paper up until two years ago when she founded the school paper—she breathed a sigh of relief. Here, it all made a bit more sense. She could write about the world's issues, share anecdotes and stories, even a poem here and there, and of course, cover school news. Behind her, the door swung open. She turned to face Carolyn Van Wooten, the retired columnist who volunteered her time as a part-time journalism instructor. From her wild, curly hair to her oversized glasses, eccentric purse covered in zebras, and her giant coffee mug, Carter couldn't help but love everything about the woman.

More than anything, when no one else stepped up to oversee the newspaper, Carolyn had come out of retirement just to support it as a pet project. Carter smiled, thinking back on the school board meeting where Carolyn had presented on the importance of teaching journalism, in fostering the spark inside a student that could change the world, and how journalism could, in fact, be the gateway to that positive change.

"Good afternoon, Carter," she said, mimicking a tip of the hat. "What's the latest word on the street?"

"I have a short blurb on the dance in two weeks, a preview of Thursday's game, the announcement of scholarship deadlines, and a column," she said, listing each one on her fingers as she spoke.

"My, what a busy day! Let's see what you have so far."

Carter handed her the printouts on the dance and scholarship deadlines. "Still working on the column and the game preview. I should have those by the end of class."

Carolyn looked at the papers, and then pulled them back and squinted over the top of her glasses. "Carry on," she said, smiling as she stepped to the makeshift desk in the corner and took her seat, sipping her coffee while she perused the articles.

Carter powered on her computer and sat, waiting while the computer went through its startup process. She'd sorted through a bunch of options for her column earlier in the week. She even had them scrawled into the notebook in her bag, but none of them seemed sufficient today.

She stretched her neck side to side and opened up her word processor. Who knew if anyone really even read what she wrote? Sure, Aiden did. A handful of the kids from the English class did, and the sports teams got excited when their pictures made the front page, but aside from that, she wasn't sure if anyone took anything meaningful from the columns.

Regardless, she had a job to do. Closing her eyes, she remembered the fervor with which she'd fought to make this a reality. It didn't matter if it meant something to a few of them or to all of them. She was going to use her platform to write and write well.

She took a deep breath, her fingers hovering above the keyboard. She had a deadline. It didn't matter if she had created the deadline or not. She was going to meet it. As she thought back through the past twenty-four hours, a subject solidified in her mind. She started to type, but she couldn't stop thinking about the situation with Logan. First Carter's staring, then Logan's, and now the upcoming game. There was so much awkwardness, and really, it didn't need to be there. She tried to push the thoughts away and focus, but they wouldn't budge. She decided she'd do what she always did—channel the thoughts for inspiration.

Twenty minutes later, she printed the document and walked it over to Carolyn's desk, where Carolyn was now playing Candy Crush on her phone. Carter stifled a giggle. She couldn't blame her. Carolyn was doing Carter a huge favor just by being here. On most days, she had lessons and lectures, but on deadline days, there was nothing for her to do but read, edit, and approve. There was a lot of waiting in the interim period.

"Hmm, I like the headline already," Carolyn said, grinning as she held the paper in her hand. "'Embracing the Discomfort of Being Awkward.' That's good stuff. You know, one of these days, I'm going to see your name splashed across one of the big national papers." She paused and took a sip of her coffee, before leveling her gaze. "And not for doing something incredibly stupid, like I'd be saying of some of your peers."

"Thank you," Carter said, laughing as she returned to her seat to type up the game preview. The matchup against Gallup was sure to be a good one, with Gallup—the reigning Five-A state champion team—having four of their five returning starters back for the year. But it wasn't a guaranteed blowout. The Cougars had played them closely each meeting last year, and with Logan and her teammate Selena really showing promise in the first couple of games of the year, it was anyone's ballgame.

She typed the article quickly, smiling as she wrote. She might not have looked the part, but she loved sports—definitely watching and not playing. It was the one thing she and her father had bonded over back in the day before he set out for his new life, wherever he was, and it made for a well-rounded writer to have varied interests. As she finished and hit Save, she reread the content one more time. She would have been excited about Thursday even before she knew she was going to be the one responsible for delivering the star of the show to the gym. Now, she was excited and nervous. Scrolling through her reel of photographs, she selected one of Logan.

Was it too obvious? Maybe. But she was the main focal point of the article. She clicked through her other options. She could put one of Selena driving to the basket that she had saved from the last game, but it didn't fit with the flow. She chewed on her lip and scrolled between the two photos.

Behind her, she heard Carolyn clear her throat. "What are you debating?"

"Just looking for the right photo," she said, moving out of the way, so Carolyn could inspect the options.

"Obviously you've got to go with Watts," Carolyn said, pointing to the picture of Logan. "Now, about your column." She leaned against the desk and crossed her arms over her chest.

"Oh, was it that bad?"

Carolyn chuckled. "No. It was that good. Are you a therapist on the side or something?"

"Just a girl with an overactive brain and a therapist mother."

"Sounds like she's one heck of a therapist and mother," Carolyn said, handing the pages back to Carter. "I like it." She paused and looked around the room. "I'm training you like a modern journalist. Do it all. Shoot your photos, write your story, lay out your page. And"—she paused to walk back over to her desk and grab her coffee cup—"you're doing a fine job. Let's go to print."

CHAPTER FOUR

Billie Eilish blared through her headphones as Logan made her way to the parking lot. She pulled her hood over her head, thankful for the light of the luminarias that the school had put up. The small paper lanterns were illuminated with candlelight inside and lined walkways throughout the city. They were traditional New Mexico Christmas decorations she'd seen a million times, but still loved. As a kid, they'd made her believe in holiday magic. Now, they served a purpose.

"Festive and useful," she mumbled to herself, as she searched for Ben's car in the parking lot. She saw the fumes of his exhaust and was grateful that he'd hung around for her a half hour after his practice had ended, and even more grateful that the car would be warmer than it was outside. For early December, it was already far colder than most winters.

"Hop in," Ben called through the cracked window. "Dad ordered Saggio's for dinner."

Logan's mouth watered at the mention of her favorite pizza place. "Nice," she said, hopping into the passenger side. "Who knew Mom being out of town would mean dinner would be awesome all the time?"

"Right? By the way, have you talked to her lately? She called me after practice and said to tell you 'hi.'"

"I'll call her later," she said, as she stole his auxiliary cord and put her music on, instead of his.

"Hey, I was listening to that," he said, scowling at her.

"And I was listening to this," she said, moving her body to the words of "bad guy."

"You've listened to this song at least a million times. It came out years ago. It's old now," he said, shaking his head. "But I'll let it slide this one time." He laughed. "This is *my* car though, and I should get to pick the music at least part of the time."

"Well, I am older. Indulge me for a bit."

"Indulge you and chauffeur you. Got it. I know my place," he said, jokingly performing a half bow, before putting the car in gear.

She turned up the music and smiled at him. He did indulge her, more often than he probably should have, but she was grateful for it. He was the only one who didn't ask more from her, didn't push her to be something she wasn't, and didn't question that she always needed a ride. As far as best friends went, it might have been lame to say it was her brother, but he definitely fit the part.

As he turned onto their street, she stared at their house and smiled. Despite the long hours her dad had been spending on the big criminal case he was prosecuting, he'd still managed somehow to string up lights and toss an inflatable reindeer in the yard.

"When did he do all this?" she asked, pointing in front of the car at their two-story adobe, now lit up like Santa's workshop.

"No clue." Ben put the car in park and took a second to admire the lights. "Got to hand it to the guy, he's like a big kid sometimes. But, I think he's really going the extra effort with Mom gone."

"Yeah." She turned to smile at him in wonder. He really was smart and compassionate beyond his years. Maybe early trauma would do that to someone. She shrugged off the dark thought. "How is Grandma, by the way? Did Mom say anything?"

"Nothing new to report, other than she's awake now."

Logan nodded, grabbing her things out of the back seat. She probably should have called her mom and at least checked in, but she couldn't bring herself to do it. As much as she loved her grandma, she didn't want to think about the inevitable. A fall at seventy-five, on top of the cancer she'd been fighting, didn't really make for a good combo.

"Hey, how was school?" Her dad stood in the doorway, waving like they were two kindergartners getting off the bus, but she didn't mind. For a second, she stopped to savor the moment. His tall, broad-shouldered frame filled the doorway, and he looked every bit as cheery as he did cold, with his thick plaid flannel and wool-lined denim jacket. In that moment, he looked so unlike the lawyer who wore suits and ties every day of his life. He just looked like a teddy bear of a dad. Ben was talking a mile a minute, filling their dad in on all the details of his day, so unlike every teen she'd ever met, so she took her time gathering her things.

She wasn't the model kid like Ben, at least not in terms of chattiness or seeing the big picture, but after all they'd been through, she did appreciate the importance of family. She'd have given anything to capture the pure joy of the moment and save it for those times when the emptiness came crashing down around her.

"Come on in, kiddo," her dad called, holding the door open. "Do you need help with your bags?"

"You make it sound like I'm moving back in," she said with a laugh.

"You practically do every day. Book bag, gym bag, makeup bag." He laughed, hugging her as she walked past. "It's like you take a mini vacation every day."

"This," she said, looking around as she dropped her bags by the doorway, "is the vacation. That place—well, aside from the court—is work."

"I know the feeling," he said, shutting the door behind her and making his way to the kitchen.

"I like the lights, by the way," she called out, not wanting to damper his obvious pride at his day's work.

"Thanks," he said, setting the pizza box on the dining room table. "We had an early recess today, waiting on a crucial piece of evidence, so I took advantage of a little time around here." He placed a stack of paper plates and napkins on the table and nodded to the chair across from his. "Have a seat. Got your favorite."

"Thank you." She took a seat and grabbed a plate, opening up the box and grabbing a thick slice of pepperoni, green chile, and olive.

As they ate, Ben entertained them with a play-by-play of his basketball practice. He wasn't in the starting lineup yet, but even as a sophomore, he was going to be a force to be reckoned with.

"What about you?" Her dad turned to face her. "You ready for the game Thursday?"

Ben smirked across the table, and she knew that he knew. She locked eyes with him for a second, and he shook his head. Her secret was safe for now, and there was no reason to bring her parents into the mess. "Ready as I'll ever be. I really think we'll get them this year. No more of them doing a clean sweep. Last year, they beat us all three times. But not this year."

"I like it," he said, taking a bite of his pizza. "I really wish I could be there, or at least send your mom to film."

"I know." She wiped her mouth with a napkin, buying a bit of time to steel her emotions. "Don't even worry about it." It was a big deal, and they all knew it. For years, her parents had traveled to every single game, and if her dad couldn't make it, he'd watch the film with her later. But, traditions were made to be broken. "Mom's where she needs to be right now."

"I know. I just hate to miss it."

"Don't stress about it, Dad." She picked up another slice. "I'll fill you in on all the highlights."

"Deal."

When they finished eating, she grabbed the box and the paper plates. "I'll do dishes tonight, Ben. Tomorrow's on you," she said, playfully nudging his shoulder. As she put the plates in the trash can, her phone buzzed in her pocket.

"I'm going to do homework," she called out, grabbing her backpack and making a beeline for her door. As much as she loved them, she needed some time alone to process her thoughts. Although it seemed like a mostly normal day, everything had been weird, from calculus class on throughout the rest of the day. Once she shut the door behind her, she grabbed her phone and opened the text from a number she hadn't saved.

Hey, it's Carter. Just shooting you a text so you have my number. See you Thursday.

Logan saved the number and started to text back. Was it weird to text back, or was it just the nice thing to do? Up until today, she hadn't given Carter a lot of thought, but she really was a nice person. Nice *and* stylish, Logan remembered, thinking back to how cute she looked in her beanie and flannel with those glasses that made her look like she belonged in a coffee shop in Oregon or something, rather than in the halls of Albuquerque Prep, milling around like the rest of the average joes.

Hey! Thanks. I'll save your number. Looking forward to it.

She hit Send before she could overthink it too much. Her phone buzzed again, and she was disappointed to see that it was Barrett. She pushed aside the notification, not wanting to show that she'd read the message, but another one came in right behind it.

She sighed and opened the message.

Want to meet up?

A few of us are headed to the Bosque to hang out.

She started to type a response, but he was already typing again. She erased her reply and waited.

It'll be fun. He'd added a winking emoji.

She really wasn't in the mood. Some nights, the Bosque was great. It was cold enough outside, no one else would be near the river and trails. They'd all meet up, probably post some stupid photos online, and half the people would end up hooking up with someone, while she'd end up home right before curfew.

Even though she wasn't quite as wild as some of the group, some nights the gatherings were fun. Tonight, she just wanted some peace and quiet. She wanted to figure out what it was that had made Barrett react so strongly this morning. He always reacted strongly, but he had no reason to really think she was a lesbian. She shook her head, trying to get his expression of disgust out of her mind.

Can't. Dad's home and insisting I finish homework.

The lie came easily. She could have probably asked her dad and he would have okayed it, but she wasn't going to take that risk.

As her phone buzzed again, she picked it up with fresh irritation. "What do you want?" she muttered, scowling at the screen, only for it to fade into a smile.

Me too. What kind of music do you like to listen to?

She leaned back on her pillows, staring at the Sue Bird poster on the back of her bedroom door. Pondering the question, she debated how to respond. She didn't want to come off as pushy and insist on her music being played, not while Carter was already driving her to the game. But, Carter *had* asked.

I like a little bit of everything. Almost always have Billie Eilish on repeat, but I've been into a lot of different things lately. Halsey, Dua Lipa, The Weeknd, some old school jams like blink-182 and Foo Fighters, and some even older stuff like Fleetwood Mac. I'll also sing along with everything from Crime Mob to Brandi Carlile. You?

She reread the message twice before sending. She should have probably added a few more obscure bands to come across cooler, but she liked what she liked. When the bubbles popped up on the screen showing that Carter was typing, she smiled again. What kind of music did Carter like? What did she like to do? Logan shook her head. She'd never really thought about it. Maybe she should widen her circle from time to time. She was always surrounded by the same people, and with college just a year away, it wouldn't hurt to try her hand at making a new friend—especially with someone who didn't just hang around the same twelve people all the time.

All good choices. I like a lot of those too, as well as the Beatles, the Black Keys, Childish Gambino, Meg Myers, Little Comets, Adaline, Fletcher, and Sharon Van Etten. I'll make a playlist.

This girl was too much, in a good way. Driving her and making a playlist.

Cool! I'll bring snacks. Any favorites?

It was the least she could offer, after all Carter was doing for her. She was really coming in clutch with getting her there when no one else could. What would they talk about for two hours? Logan closed her eyes and tried to imagine the ride, but decided between music and snacks, they'd have plenty to focus on. If nothing else, they could always turn the music up loud.

Gummy bears and coffee, the secret to any successful journalistic endeavor.

Logan laughed out loud, propping herself up on another pillow.

I think it's pretty cool you do the school paper stuff. I love your columns.

Really? I wasn't sure anyone ever read them.

I really do enjoy them. There's a lot of cool inspirational stuff in there. She looked to her nightstand, where she knew she'd stashed a couple that had helped her through some of her darkest days of depression. That was too much to admit. She hit Send.

Thanks! I'm really glad to hear that. By the way, I'm sure you're going to crush it Thursday. I wrote an entire article about it.

Logan felt her cheeks grow hot. It was no secret that she was one of the lead scorers of the team, but even though Carter was covering the game, she didn't really think she would have been a fan.

Thanks! You like basketball?

Love it! My dad and I watched it all the time growing up. It was one of the few things we had in common.

This girl was full of surprises.

Who's your favorite team?

That depends on the league. WNBA – Washington Mystics, because Elena Delle Donne is a queen. NBA – San Antonio Spurs. NCAA Women's – Tennessee. NCAA Men's – Duke.

Quite the spread! I like it!

Logan breathed a sigh of relief. She'd had her doubts. It had been years since she'd made a new friend, and even then, it was a friend who was pulled into her existing group of friends. But, this was going to be okay. They'd have plenty to talk about on Thursday. Logan glanced at her backpack. She really should be doing her chemistry homework, especially after dozing off. She grabbed the book from her bag, along with a notebook. All she wanted to do was continue this lighthearted conversation, but she was already in enough trouble.

I've got to catch up on some stuff for chemistry. She typed her response, wanting to add more, but a quick glance at the clock told her she was already biting off more than she could chew. *I'll be sure and bring the good snacks on Thursday!*

She set her phone on her nightstand to get the distraction out of her mind. The phone lit up continuously with messages from Barrett, Selena, Josie, and everyone she assumed was out at the Bosque. She flipped the phone over to cover the screen. But even as she settled in to work on her homework, she couldn't help but think that what had started off as a punishment might actually turn into something fun.

CHAPTER FIVE

Around her, lockers clanged shut and kids chattered loudly as if finally freed from the prison of the school day. Carter downed the kombucha she'd treated herself to after her last class of the day. Normally, she'd have been on the road already, getting to the opposing team's gym early enough to set up all of her equipment, test shoot a couple of warm-up photos and cover the junior varsity game, but today that wasn't her focus.

She'd wait the extra half hour for Logan to finish up. Making her way to the bathroom, she examined her outfit for probably the thirtieth time of the day. Not that it should have mattered, but she wanted to look the part of both journalist and maybe cool new friend. She rolled her eyes at her reflection. She had plenty of friends, but this one was different. This new friendship meant paving the path to actually meeting new people and breaking outside of her comfort zone. And, more than that, it meant hanging out with Logan Watts, someone she'd all but worshipped the past couple of years. Carter's black jeans hugged her curves in all the right places, she noted. These would go in her college pile for when she was actually trying to get dates. The white shirt she'd chosen popped perfectly against the steel gray scarf and denim jacket she'd paired it with. She looked down at her Chucks and gave herself a mental high five.

It all screamed lesbian journalist on the town—the exact look she was going for when she'd started the day. The only thing missing was a giant cup of coffee, which she hoped Logan had remembered to bring. In the car, she'd add her beanie for an extra touch. If there was such a thing as too many accessories, she hadn't gotten that memo. She smiled, knowing she'd have tossed the memo in the trash, right alongside everything else people told her she just *had* to do.

She pulled her glasses off to clean the lenses. As she wiped them on the hem of her shirt, she smiled. Today felt different. It wasn't just a normal day. It was a fresh start.

"Here you go again, getting poetic," she whispered to herself, shaking her head, but knowing it was true. Regardless of how cheesy it felt to admit, something was different, in a good way.

She opened her phone, flipping over to her Spotify account and checking to make sure the playlist had saved. It might have been over-the-top, but she wanted to make Logan feel at ease. Nothing did that more quickly than music.

Music is therapy. She'd repeated the mantra a million times, and it was just as true every time she said it.

With a few minutes left until Logan finished up, Carter went to her car, started the engine, and pulled to the front of the school. Once she found a parking spot, long since abandoned by any of the students who showed up early enough to get front row parking, she shot Logan a quick text.

Out front. You can't miss me. I'm in the Honda Civic that's older than both of us. She added an emoji and plugged in her phone to the charger. She looked around the car. She'd taken the time to vacuum the interior and added one of those air fresheners that looked like a pine tree. If nothing else, it added to the car's vintage vibes.

"It's your time to shine, Sophia," she said, affectionately patting the dash of her car, named after her favorite Golden

Girl. "This is the first of many adventures I shall take you on, where you'll be responsible for impressing the ladies." She laughed at the thought, but cleared her throat as she saw Logan emerge from the building. Game day was always a treat, since the coaches insisted that the players dress up to look professional before traveling. Instead of her normal jeans and a hoodie, Logan wore fitted gray slacks and a navy blue button-down covered in a pattern of prints of some sort of bird. Whatever they were, Carter was willing to call them her favorite animal. The ensemble was a striking look on Logan's tall, slender frame. She smiled as she spotted Carter. Greeting her with a nod, she walked over and tossed her bags in the back seat. Neatly hanging her jersey on the hook, she rounded the car toward the passenger side.

"I didn't forget," she said, as she climbed inside. Reaching behind her, she pulled out a giant bag of gummy bears and two bottled coffees. "It's not fresh, but I didn't have time to grab you something hot. I hope this is okay."

She held the snacks out, as if they were a peace offering. Her sheepish grin made Carter smile. "This is perfect. Thank you." She accepted the bag of gummy bears, opened it up, and put it in the console between the seats. "Help yourself."

"Thanks," Logan said, grabbing a few bears from the bag. "I figured we have two hours, so we needed the jumbo bag." She grinned as she popped one in her mouth. "There's another bag for you, by the way, for the ride home. I'll be back on the bus then, but I didn't want to leave you without any company."

Carter smiled, but her heart fell. She'd forgotten all about the ride home. Not that she didn't enjoy her alone time, but today wasn't about solitude. She straightened her shoulders, intent not to let any negative emotions seep through and ruin their time. She had plenty of time to brood on the way home, if needed. For now, she'd live in the moment. And the moment just happened to have coffee, gummy bears, and Logan Watts.

Beside her, Logan leaned back in her seat and popped open her metal reusable water bottle, which Carter was now close enough to see was covered in an array of stickers, ranging from bands to pop culture references, to motivational quotes, to a llama. She stifled a laugh, while Logan took a long swig.

When Logan screwed the cap back on, she glanced over at Carter. "So what's first on the playlist? I hope you included some of your music. I hadn't heard of some of the bands before, and I'm always down to expand my horizons."

Carter laughed, nervously turning up the music. "I took some liberties with it," she said, putting the car in gear. "I hope you like it. Think of it as your very own Tiny Desk Concert."

"Tiny Desk?" Logan crinkled her nose, and Carter looked away, focusing her eyes on the road. Logan's expressions were so distracting, she was sure she'd crash if she didn't pay more attention.

"It's a regular show on NPR." She took a drink of the coffee and waited for a response. "Public radio," she clarified when Logan didn't respond.

"Oh, cool! Well, I'm looking forward to my musical awakening."

Out of the corner of her eye, Carter watched as Logan moved her head to the beat. "I like this one," she said after a couple of minutes. "It's got a chill vibe. Really nice," she added, grabbing another gummy bear.

"Good, I'm glad." Carter winked. She gulped. She could have kicked herself. What was she doing winking?

"So, Carter Shaw," Logan said, clearing her throat. The way Logan said her name, it sounded as sweet as honey. Carter fought to keep a neutral expression. She was going to have to get it together, considering this was as close to a date as she'd dared to go on thus far, and it was absolutely *not* a date. Logan was straight. She shouldn't have to keep reminding herself of that fact. "Why is it that our paths have never crossed before?"

Carter gave her a sideways glance. "Really?"

"I mean, I know we've had our share of classes together, but aside from that, we've never hung out or anything." Logan shrugged. "You have good taste in music and snacks, and you're fun to talk to."

"Don't spread that around school," Carter said dryly, grabbing another gummy bear for herself.

"Oh, so is that it?" Logan narrowed her eyes, studying Carter as if she was a foreign object. "You don't really like people?"

"Not *all* people." Carter laughed. "It's just that we hang in different circles."

"I guess I never really thought too hard about the circles."

"You didn't have to," Carter challenged gently. "You can go say 'hi' to anyone in the halls, and no one is going to look at you like you have a third eye."

"A third eye, like in a spiritual type of way?" Logan's laugh made Carter smile.

"You know what I mean."

"I do," Logan said, taking a long sip of her water. For a second, she gazed out the passenger side window, and Carter wished she knew what was going on inside her head. "For the record, you could have always come up to say 'hi' to me. I think you're cool. But, I probably should have always known I could come up and say 'hi' to you too." She looked out the window again, and then turned in her seat so she faced Carter. "Either way, I'm really glad we're hanging out now. Thanks again for driving me."

"Yeah, no problem. I'm glad too." She considered saying more, but let the comfortable silence ride for a few minutes.

As the music switched over to a blink-182 song, she watched as Logan's smile grew. "This one is my favorite," she said, dancing to the beat. Logan reached over and turned up the volume, singing along to every word. Carter sang along too, watching as Logan exuded the confidence she envied. She was sure of herself and knew her place in the world, but to be so comfortable in her skin that she'd hop in a stranger's car and belt out a song at the top of her lungs was something Carter could only imagine came from a lifetime of excelling at everything she attempted.

Acing tests? Effortless. Breaking scoring records? She made it look easy. Attracting a crowd of people who watched her every move? She'd had that in the bag probably since she entered the world. Carter bit her lip, looking down at her lap momentarily. She shouldn't be so callous. She knew as well as anyone did that even popularity, looks, and athletic skills didn't protect you from tragedy. Logan had suffered her fair share.

As the song came to a close, she offered Logan a smile. "Glad to see I got it right."

"Nailed it!" Logan said, offering up her hand for a high five.

Carter smacked her hand against Logan's, the contact making her heart beat faster.

"So I know you have a crew you run with," Logan said, leaning back in her chair dramatically, like she'd just performed a concert for adoring fans, which she kind of did, if you considered a concert for an audience of one. A private concert. Carter blushed at the thought. "What do you do for fun?"

"Same thing most people do I guess." Carter chewed on a gummy bear, buying herself a minute. She wanted to sound interesting, maybe more interesting than she really was. She swallowed. "We hang out at the mall, hike the nature trails, go to Lobo games, and all that stuff. I write a lot in my spare time."

"Yeah!" Logan's enthusiastic response made her laugh nervously. "I wanted to talk to you more about that. Where do you get your material?"

"Overactive imagination, I guess." Carter tapped her fingers on the steering wheel. "My mom says I'm always in my head. Have been since I was a kid. And, my mom is a therapist, so she's always been big on mental health and self-awareness. I guess it kind of rubbed off on me."

"I think it's fantastic. I couldn't write like that."

"You have an A in honors English," Carter said, dismissing Logan's compliment.

"That's for stuff I have to write. If I was pressed to come up with something just off the cuff, I think I'd fall flat on my face."

"Well, thank you," Carter conceded. "Same goes for me and sports though. As much as I love to follow the game, toss a ball in my direction, and I'd drop the pass every time."

Logan laughed. "I guess we both have our strengths. Speaking of which, I know you said you liked Lobo games. If you're sticking around in the area, you can come watch me ride the bench next year."

Carter coughed, choking on the gummy bear she'd been eating. She cleared her throat. "Yeah, I'd love that, but I'm sure you won't be on the bench."

"I'll be a freshman." Logan pursed her lips. "I've been a big fish in a little pond for a while. The game changes at the next level. I'm sure I'll do my time and pay my dues like everyone else."

"You're going to blow off being the only high school player in the state to score one hundred and twenty-seven three pointers in a season…as a *junior*!"

Logan leaned back and looked at Carter. She opened her mouth and shook her head. "You know my stats? Like the exact number?"

"Photographic memory," Carter said, shrugging off the attention. "I have to keep an eye on things to report them."

"Oh right," Logan said, laughing. "Sorry. I was about to say, I think you might have my dad beat out on being my number one fan."

Carter's mouth ran dry from Logan's words. "I…" She laughed. "I mean, I didn't say I'm not a fan."

"Thanks," Logan said with a good-natured smile. "Didn't mean to put you on the spot."

What did she mean by that? Carter's mind raced with possibilities. Was she being too flirty? Or was it obvious that she *was* a big fan. It was already out in the open that she liked the game of basketball, but she didn't want to come across like the overly obsessed fan for other reasons. She'd be the first to admit that she enjoyed the games for their sheer athleticism, but she was also honest enough to admit to herself that female athletes were undoubtedly her type. That was, if she even had a type. Could you have a type without ever having a girlfriend? She'd had a fling, but nothing more. Did she have a type? Who would she have picked to ask to the upcoming dance, if she had the chance?

"So…" Logan said, drawing out the word. "Are you going to the big dance in a couple of weeks?"

"What?" Carter asked, glancing over at Logan with what she knew was sheer terror on her face. It was as if Logan was reading her mind. She gripped the steering wheel and gulped, straightening her shoulders. "Yeah, I'll be there," she said, composing herself. "Have to cover it for the paper."

"Are you taking anyone?"

Carter grabbed the bottle of coffee and chugged the remaining contents, suddenly unsure if it was a good idea to have invited someone else into her bubble of safety.

"No," she managed after swallowing. "I'll be flying solo, like always."

"Why is that?" Logan stopped a gummy bear halfway to her mouth. "Never mind. You don't have to answer that. Is that an insensitive question? And of course, it's fine if you just don't want to date. Or if there aren't any good prospects, or…I'm going to shut up now." Logan stuffed a gummy bear in her mouth, and in an instant, gone was the cool and confident person from just seconds before.

Glad to know she wasn't the only one who could easily get so flustered, Carter laughed. "It's fine," she said, reaching out and patting Logan's shoulder. She jerked her hand back almost as soon as she made contact. That didn't make things less weird. She cleared her throat. "There are definitely fewer prospects for me to choose from than for others at school. I just kind of figured I'd wait until college and then try to start dating then." Logan was studying her intently, hanging on every word, so she took a deep breath. She really didn't get into all of this aside from with Aiden, but they still had an hour and a half left to drive. "I'm pretty sure there's only a couple of other kids who are even out at school," she said, as she considered what all she should or shouldn't say. "There really aren't a lot of options, and even if there were, I just don't know that I'd want the whole high school romance thing for me, especially this late in the game."

"What do you mean?"

"There's the whole concept of having to break up or do long distance if you go to different colleges, and I'd never dream of going to the same college as someone just because we dated in high school."

"That's a good point," Logan said. She clasped her hands together and then started playing with her cuticles. Biting her lip, she let out a sigh. "I never really thought about that."

"About the lesbian dating prospects at our school, or about breaking up after graduation."

"Both." Logan chewed on a fingernail, before stopping and straightening her shoulders as though she'd been caught doing something she wasn't supposed to do. "I guess I just really never expected my relationship with Barrett to last as long as it has, so I never really thought about the whole dating after high school thing."

The way she spoke the words with such a coolness, almost as if there was no emotion tied to it, threw Carter for a loop. "You've been together for three years, which in high school time, is like a decade."

"True," Logan said, casting her attention down to the gummy bears in her hand, before carefully selecting a red one to pop into her mouth. She chewed slowly, and Carter could only imagine she was deep in contemplation. When she swallowed, she turned to Carter. "I probably shouldn't be saying all this, but you're my new friend, right?" She smiled, looking every bit like a kid on Christmas morning, about to receive a present.

"Right," Carter said, basking in the sunlight of that smile directed at her.

"Cool." Logan crossed her arms over her chest. "Thing is… this can't leave this car. Deal?"

Carter nodded.

"Good." Logan took a deep breath. "I don't get the whole dating thing, I guess."

"What?" Carter tried to keep the astonishment out of her voice, but failed. "You've been dating forever."

"Yeah," Logan said, waving a hand through the air, "but not like the way some people do. Like, half the girls just won't stop talking about their boyfriends and always want them around, and I just don't get it. Maybe that's why I've never really thought of the breakup aspect of things."

"Do you not love him?" The question came out before she could stop it, and she wished she could snatch it back out of the air, judging by the scowl on Logan's face.

Expecting a retort of some sort, she watched as Logan's shoulders fell and she leaned back against the seat.

CHAPTER SIX

Love. The word hung in the air like a thick fog. Carter had already changed the subject, talking about how she'd gone to see the Black Keys in concert in Taos once, and how amazing their performance was. Logan nodded along and added a comment here and there, even though she'd all but since stopped listening.

Did she love Barrett? How could she know really? Sure, she said it before. It felt like the thing she was supposed to do. Everyone said it when they'd been dating a while. There wasn't usually a need to question it. After all, if Carter was right, they'd just be breaking up anyway, so what was the point? She chewed off the nail of her right index finger and silently chided herself. She was supposed to be overcoming that bad habit, but really, who did it hurt?

"What's wrong?"

"With me?" Logan squeaked. Clearing her throat, she deepened her voice. "Nothing. Why?"

"You've been heavy sighing for the last ten minutes, and you just ripped off a hunk of your nail like it was nothing."

"Oh," Logan said, looking down at her lap. "A bad habit I've had since I was a kid, despite my mother's best efforts." She offered a smile. "I think I'm just nervous about the game."

"You get pregame jitters?" Carter narrowed her eyes, seeing past her lie.

"From time to time." She always got them, just not usually before they got to the gym.

"What is it really? Did I upset you with my question earlier?"

"No." Logan shook her head. "You didn't upset me. I was just lost in my head. I have a tendency of doing that."

"I do the same thing," Carter said, keeping her tone light. "If I've learned anything through reading far too many therapy books, it's that it's okay to talk about the things going on up there."

Logan bit her lip. Normally, she'd shut her mouth and move on, but something in Carter's kind smile inexplicably prompted her to move forward. "Maybe I'm just defective or something. I don't even know how I'd know if I loved him." She shifted in her seat. "Have you ever been in love?"

Carter stiffened and shook her head. "No. I have not, but I have had my share of crushes, and one brief encounter that didn't even really count as a date or relationship."

Logan had so many questions. Who? Anyone she knew? This was already too personal though, so she thought through the appropriate responses. "How did you know you liked them?"

"Most of the typical things." Carter kept her eyes glued to the road, but her voice dropped an octave. "Mainly, I know when I keep thinking about them constantly, or I hope they're having a good day. I want to learn all about them, see what really makes them tick, you know?" She ran her tongue across her lips as if thinking about her next words carefully, and Logan's eyes followed the movement. Even her lipstick was the perfect shade to match every bit of her quirky style. Logan fixated on her mouth, watching as she spoke. Her full lips seemed to punctuate every word. Logan straightened in her seat. She was doing it again, the staring thing. "I want to hear from them. I want to hang out with them. I want to make them laugh. I miss their company when they're not around. All those little things. That's how I know."

"Hmm. I guess maybe I haven't felt that." Logan replayed it all. She liked hanging out with Barrett, but mostly didn't miss him when he was gone. And, he certainly texted too often.

"That's okay too. You know, some people are asexual, and there's nothing wrong with that."

"I don't think I'm asexual," Logan said, contemplating the word as she spoke it. That certainly wasn't it. She wanted to date, possibly even to have sex one day, but not with Barrett. The thought made her grimace. "I should really break up with him," she muttered. "Shit, sorry. I shouldn't have said that out loud."

Carter's laughter filled the air. "This is a safe space. I won't say anything. Besides, you know I don't talk to anyone in your crowd anyway." Carter reached out as though she was going to comfort Logan but quickly pulled back, placing her hands perfectly at the ten and two positions on the steering wheel. "From what I've heard, high school is all about figuring out what you want anyway, and then college is really the time to explore that."

"And have you done that?"

"Figured out what I want?" Carter knitted her brow. "In some abstract way, I guess. I've just never put it into practice."

"So you've never dated?"

Carter shook her head.

"Never kissed anyone?"

"I didn't say that." Carter raised an eyebrow and smiled. "I just said I've never dated."

The wheels in Logan's mind churned. "Boy? Girl? Both?"

"Both," Carter said, her voice barely above a whisper.

Maybe she'd crossed a line, but her curiosity was piqued. "What is that like?"

"Kissing?" Carter eyed her carefully and then nodded. "Ah, what's kissing a girl like?"

Logan nodded, speechless. She'd never really contemplated the fact that it might be different.

"It's still just kissing, but somehow softer, more intimate. But also, more passionate." She paused and looked at Logan. "That's just for me though, I'm sure. You know, since I like girls and don't have those same feelings for guys."

"Gotcha." Logan nodded, trying to process all the information. It wasn't that she was an alien and hadn't heard of same-sex couples. As a huge WNBA fan, several of her heroes were in the LGBTQ community, but she'd just never really sat down and talked to someone about it. She watched as Carter pressed the second bottle of coffee to her lips and wondered what they'd feel like. Maybe they really were softer than Barrett's sloppy kisses. She diverted her attention, looking out the window. There was no reason she should even be considering the thought. She had a boyfriend, even if she was questioning whether she even liked him, based off Carter's definition.

She crossed her arms and leaned against the cool glass. Why was she with him anyway? She thought back to three years ago, when he'd first asked her out. It just seemed right, two up-and-coming athletes being side by side all the time. He was handsome, and even funny when he wasn't trying to impress his football teammates. But was that all there was to it? She thought back to the dates, the group get-togethers, and had to wonder if it was all that shallow.

"You said you knew what you wanted," Logan said, breaking the silence. "What is that? If you could build your perfect girl, what would she be like?"

Carter smiled and took a deep breath. Keeping her eyes on the road, she swallowed hard. "Well, she'd be a lot of things, too complex to figure out in most ways, but I know she'd have a good sense of humor, she'd put me at ease and make me feel like I was home, and she'd be smart and would have dreams and goals. She'd support my dreams too, and…" Carter trailed off and looked out the driver's side window, before turning briefly to Logan. "She'd be pretty and probably athletic. She'd like music and reading." She ran her finger across her lower lip. "Those are the basics."

"She sounds like a badass, but she'd have to be to land you," Logan said, looking Carter up and down. "Really, you're pretty much the whole package."

Carter's cheeks blushed, and she lowered her head with a grin. "Thanks," she said. "I am a Scorpio though, if that's a game changer in the total package department."

"Happy late birthday in that case," Logan said, laughing. "I'm a Leo, so I don't know that I'm much better."

"I know, August seventeenth," Carter said, before glancing down at her phone in the console. "Looks like we've got about ten minutes left. Anything else you want to know?"

Everything. Logan wanted to know everything, but she couldn't say that. "Why don't we hang out again sometime soon? I've enjoyed talking, and even if I said too much, I'd like to do it again."

Carter's smile grew, and she nodded. "Sure. Just let me know."

"I will." She glanced at her gym bag in the back seat and refocused her energy. Tonight was a big night, and it wouldn't serve her well to be in her head before they got to the gym.

"Anything you usually do pregame that'll help you get in the zone?" Carter asked, as though she could read her mind.

"I usually just prep a bit by running through what I know of the opposing team, and then shake out all the jitters once I get on the court for warm-ups." She reached in her bag and pulled out a couple of Tylenol, popping them in her mouth and swallowing them with a drink of water.

"What are those for?"

"Nothing." Logan offered a smile.

"Are you okay?"

Logan nodded, dismissing the concern. She might have trusted Carter with the intimate details of her non-romantic romantic life, but she wasn't going to get into all of her problems just yet.

"Want to run it by me?" Carter asked. "The rundown of the game, I mean."

Logan smiled, noting Carter's genuine interest. "Yeah, sure." She put one leg under her body and closed her eyes. "They're going to be tough. They always are. If I know them well, they'll double-team either me or Selena, depending on who's having a better night. That makes a tougher game for one of us, but it frees up Gabrielle to get a shot off from time to time, and she's stepped up her game this year." She stretched her neck side to side, already feeling the tension fade. "On the defensive end, I'll be matched up against the same girl I was last year—Catori Adair. I'll have my work cut out for me, if her shots are falling tonight like they were in our last couple of matchups."

"Catori doesn't like to go to the left," Carter said matter-of-factly. "You've got that going for you."

Logan eyed her with growing curiosity. "You watch the game film or something?"

"No." Carter laughed. "I've just been watching every game, and you all met three times last year, twice in regular season and once in the playoffs. You always guard her, and it's just a weakness I picked up on."

"Nice, well thanks for the tip, Coach Shaw." She playfully elbowed Carter and watched as Carter's cheeks flushed again. Logan laughed nervously. There was something so strange about sitting here, discussing basketball with someone who knew it and talked it so well, yet never played, with someone who she'd never spoken to in depth but suddenly felt like one of her oldest friends.

As they pulled into the gym, she grabbed her stuff and hopped out of the passenger seat. "Thanks again," she said, leaning over to give Carter a hug. Carter froze as Logan wrapped her arms around her, and Logan backed up quickly. "Ah, damn, are you not a hugger?"

"No." Carter shook her head. "I am. It just caught me off guard. Anyway, good luck, and text me when you want to hang out." She waved, as Logan turned to go.

* * *

Sweat dripped down Logan's brow, and the crowd roared. With two minutes to go, the game was a tie. The crowd was always loud when they came to Gallup. The rivalry was strong between the two teams, and as the defending state champs, they had a lot on the line in their first district game of the season.

Logan's heart raced from the adrenaline of it all. She ran down the court and set up in her shooting guard position. Coming down the court, Selena called out the play.

"Purple," she shouted, signifying a slight variation from their usual go-to motion offense. As Logan ran the baseline, she took her screen and popped up on the three-point line, wide open. Selena found her with ease, and she turned, sinking the bucket before her defense ever caught up.

With a smile, she sprinted back on defense. Within seconds, they passed the ball to Catori. A hand in her face, Logan shut down her chance to get a quick shot off.

"Take her to the left." She remembered Carter's comments, as well as the reminders her coach had given her in their pregame talk. Shifting her body, she forced herself between Catori's right side and the basket. Catori eyed the floor and set in motion, straight into Logan where she was planted. Behind her the whistle blew, and the official signaled an offensive foul, Catori's fifth of the game.

Jumping from the ground, Logan pumped her fist in the air as she ran to the foul line.

"One-in-one," the ref under the basket called, as he tossed the ball in Logan's direction.

She took a deep breath, dribbling the ball twice like she'd done in repetition from the time she learned to shoot a free throw. Drowning out the noise, she focused and sank the first shot.

"Cougars up by four," the announcer called out. She glanced at the clock. Less than a minute remaining.

After she sunk her second shot and Gallup called a time-out, she could feel the excitement mounting. With a five-point lead, they just had to hold them to no score in this possession and protect the ball, and the game was theirs.

They lined up for the inbound, and Logan saw her opportunity on the long lob. Launching herself in front of the ball, she got the steal and ran it back for a quick, uncontested layup.

As the clock ran out on the final seconds and they secured their first district win of the year, Logan looked up to the stands in the direction from which she'd heard Carter cheering.

Beaming, Carter stood behind her camera and snapped a picture. Logan pointed up in the stands with a nod as a silent "thank you," and headed toward the bench. Just when she thought she'd be without a cheering section of her own, Carter had stepped in to save the day, just like she had from the beginning of the week.

CHAPTER SEVEN

The upbeat sounds of Olivia Rodrigo played over her Bluetooth speaker, and Carter took another long look in the mirror. Even if it was obsessive, she wanted to look perfect tonight, for no one other than herself. She mentally repeated the mantra, even if she knew it wasn't true. Ever since that car ride, her imagination had been in a tailspin. What would it be like to have those kinds of moments with a girl who was actually into her?

More than that, what would it be like to get to hang out with Logan again? Logan, who was so much more than met the eye. Behind the cool façade of the best ball player at the school was a young woman of depth.

Young woman? She shuddered at her own use of the word. They were both eighteen, but it still didn't make the wording less creepy.

"What's taking you so long?" Aiden called out for the third time from her bedroom. "You have a hot date you didn't tell me about?"

"Just finishing up," she shouted over the music, admiring her formal blue dress once more. The way it dipped off one shoulder made her smile. She'd swept her hair back into a side up-do that was every bit as bohemian as she was hoping it would be. Finalizing the look with a pair of gold earrings in the shape of the tree of life, she shimmied for the mirror.

You're the whole package. She heard Logan's words replay in her mind and smiled at the thought. If Logan could see it, maybe someone else would some day too. In the meantime, she sure as hell saw it.

She opened the door, watching as Aiden's jaw dropped open. "Wow," he said quietly, looking her up and down. "You look amazing!"

"Why, thank you," she said, doing a mock twirl and looking him up and down. "You clean up well too, sir."

He smiled, straightening his houndstooth tie. Paired with his maroon suit, it was perfectly his style. "Let's grab some pictures with your mom, and then we'll head out. She's already run her shot list by me," he said, rolling his eyes but giving a goofy smile nonetheless. He grabbed her arm, escorting her down the stairs. "Stop here," he whispered halfway down, placing his arm around her and smiling down to the bottom, where her mom waited with a camera.

"Honey you look amazing," her mom said, wrapping her into a hug after snapping a handful of pictures. "You'd make the perfect date for any girl lucky enough to have you." Carter blushed, but offered a smile. She looked at her mom carefully, noting her beautiful light brown skin and brown eyes, some of the few traits that she'd passed down to her daughter.

Her mother was nothing if not supportive. She'd made that clear from day one, but it still didn't make Carter any more comfortable talking about it. It felt like the more they talked about it, the more she felt like she had to offer some explanation as to why she wasn't dating. It wasn't really easy to tell her mom that she kept falling for straight girls. Call it what she wanted, she already knew that was the train she was setting into motion, yet again. She mentally tallied them up. Logan would make four painful, unrequited crushes.

As she plastered on a smile for the pictures in her mother's rose garden, she reminded herself that college was a fresh start, and that she was confident in who she was—single or with someone—even if she did secretly long for that connection.

"Now a silly one," she heard her mom call out. Her laughter was contagious, lightening Carter's mood as she struck a goofy face. By the time they headed out the door, she was sure her cheeks were going to hurt from smiling for so long. It had been worth it, to see her mom's smile light up the room, but she was thankful for the reprieve.

"So how's your new BFF?" Aiden asked, once they were in the car. "Is she coming tonight on the arm of her super stud beau?"

"Why do you talk like you're fifty?" Carter asked, playfully hitting his arm. "She's not my best friend, by the way. That's you. Always has been, since that fateful day of freshman year."

"Oh no!" Aiden shook his head. "Let's not relive it."

"You with your social awkwardness, still the last to go through puberty, just looking for a bud, and me not wanting anything to do with the girls talking about which boy they found attractive. A match made in heaven."

"I'd say we turned out okay," he said, glancing in the rearview mirror.

She nodded. He was right. "You look very handsome, by the way," she reassured him. He did. There was no denying he'd overcome his gangly phase and turned into a good-looking guy. He was still every bit as awkward as he'd always been though, which was why he was taking her to the winter formal, instead of escorting an actual date.

"Thank you," he said, nodding at his reflection as if giving himself some sort of silent pep talk. "And, I'm not saying she's your *best* friend. I'm just saying the two of you have gotten pretty close."

"If by close, you mean one car ride and a handful of texts, then sure." It had been more than that, but Carter wasn't going to admit that to him. She snuck a side-glance at her phone to see if Logan had texted today. Her screen was blank, and she wished she hadn't checked.

"A handful of texts?" Aiden shook his head. "I don't know who you're hiding from, but you're always smiling at that damn thing these days." He jerked his head in her direction, and his mouth fell open. "Oh my god! You like her."

"I do not."

"Is she not as straight as we all thought? Is her relationship really a sham like I called it to be? Oh my god, are you two together?"

"Slow it down, TMZ." Carter shook her head and stared at him for added effect. "You sure jump to conclusions quickly. No, we're not together. No, she's not in a sham of a relationship." She worked hard to keep her tone neutral. She'd promised she wouldn't sell out Logan's secret. "And, yes, I believe she's straight." *Sadly*, she added silently.

"We'll see about all of that," he said, staring out the window for a second, before turning toward her. "I guess maybe I'm just being catty because I'm jealous."

"Jealous? I still spend practically every waking hour with you."

"And next year you're moving off to the big city." He faked a pouting face.

She rolled her eyes. "Truthfully, I don't know that I am. I've been thinking about it more and more, and I might just stick around here. I know Mom will be fine, but I don't know that I want to live that far from her, or from you, or from home." She contemplated the thought for the millionth time and sighed. "We'll see. Nothing is set in stone. I still love New York, but maybe I just love the idea of it."

"Well, either way, I'll come visit you there, or you and I can live together here."

"Does that mean I'm going to have to deal with all the girls you inevitably bring home, once you finally get away from the cursed high school reputation?"

"All the girls *I'm* going to bring home?" He laughed. "I think it's going to be the other way around, but either way, we'll get through college the same way we got through high school."

She offered him a quick smile, before glancing back at her phone. She'd thought all day about shooting Logan a quick text, but didn't want to make it awkward. There was no doubt, she was going to look stunning, but she was also going to be on Barrett's arm all night or surrounded by her crew of athletes and high school royalty. At least this dance didn't have a king and queen. It was such a ridiculous concept, and it was typically a bit homophobic as well. Of course, there were tons of straight couples, but it didn't mean others didn't exist. Why should it always be a girl and guy?

"You nervous or something?" Aiden asked, bringing her out of her thoughts.

"No. Sorry, was just lost down a rabbit hole of social justice."

"Well, dig your way out, because we're here." He gestured grandly at the gymnasium.

"Here goes nothing," she said, grabbing her camera bag out of the back seat.

"Are you really going to tote that thing around all night? Aren't you at least going to dance to a couple of songs?"

"I might." She put the strap over her shoulder, careful not to slip on the ice. Whoever planned formal dances in winter should have really rethought their life choices. "But I'll probably do what I always do. Sip some punch, take some photos, talk to you, talk to whoever comes by the punch table, and dance like a dad at prom from where I stand."

"Is it too early to pull out the old pepper grinder?" He mimicked the ridiculous dance move by the car. Laughing, she motioned for him to follow her.

"It's never too early for that one, but you might want to wait until someone has at least spiked the punch. Then everyone will just think you're that goofy drunk guy."

"I live for those moments."

He fell in step beside her, taking her arm as they entered. It was a superficial touch, but it felt nice not to have to enter alone. Once inside the gym, she took it all in. There were streamers and fake snowflakes all over, as if an elementary art classroom had exploded. She scanned the crowd.

"Are you looking for your new *friend*?" Aiden whispered in her ear.

"Looking for a good place to set up the camera," she lied, keeping her voice low. "Go ahead and go mingle. I'll catch up with you in a few."

He bounded off toward a group of girls huddled by the punch table. Carter's heart pounded as she zeroed in on Logan across the gym. Her long honey-colored hair trailed down her back as she playfully danced with a couple of her teammates. Her red dress shimmered in the light, and Carter was sure she'd never seen someone so stunning. Someone bumped into her, and she turned to find one of the football players already drunk.

"My bad," he said, and she scowled at the sickly sweet smell of liquor emanating from him.

She wasn't naive. She knew some of her classmates drank, and she was fine with the idea of a drink now and then, but there was something just plain sad about showing up to a high school dance already half in the bag. She moved to the side, letting him move past her, before taking a second to catch her breath. If she was going to continue to coexist with Logan Watts, Carter was going to have to remember that even if she looked like a goddess, she was a straight woman, and a friend at that. No good would come of crossing that boundary, if that was ever even an option.

She straightened her shoulders and walked toward the punch table. Choosing a vantage point from which she could capture both the door and the dance floor, she set up her tripod. Needing a test subject, she aimed her camera at the dance floor, bringing Logan's face into view. She snapped a few photos, before forcing herself to face the door and capture couples arriving. As the moments passed, she silently evaluated the dresses and suits of each couple she photographed to make the time go more quickly. There were the couples who tried too hard for a vintage vibe—bringing back the brightly colored suits of the seventies—as well as those who looked like they were practicing for a traditional white and black wedding, and everything in between.

"There you are." She heard Logan's voice behind her.

Her heart beat faster as she turned to face her. "Red is definitely your color," she stammered. Dammit. What kind of opening was that?

"Thank you," Logan said, smiling and looking at Carter's dress. "Blue suits you, as well. How've you been?"

How had she been? Crazy. Confused. Undone. "Good. I've been good. And you?"

"Really good. Sorry we haven't found a time to hang out yet." She looked back over her shoulder, where Josie was calling her name. She held up a finger, letting Josie know she'd be a minute.

"It's fine. I know you're in high demand."

"It's not that." Logan looked to the ground. Carter followed suit, taking in her white Chucks she'd paired with her dress.

"Love the shoes," she commented, showing off her own that matched.

"You have got to take a picture of that. Here," she said, extending her leg, so her foot touched against Carter's.

"Sure," Carter said, leaning back to capture the image with the camera.

"Uh, anyway," Logan said, taking a step back so she was across from Carter. "My mom's been out of town, so I've been helping out more around the house and haven't really had a lot of free time, but if you'd like, maybe we can grab a bite after the dance?"

Carter smiled, but it dissipated as Barrett came up behind her. "After the dance, we're all going to Frontier for food and then out to the Bosque. You coming?" he asked, sliding up behind Logan and placing his hands around her waist. He turned his attention to Carter. "I could buy you dinner to thank you for bringing my all-star to the game the other day."

He didn't wait for an answer and kissed Logan's cheek instead. Carter looked away and clutched her camera. "I'd love to, but I don't know that I'm going to make it."

"Not what I had in mind," Logan mouthed, shaking her head softly so as not to disturb Barrett who was too focused on his public display of one-sided affection.

Carter shrugged. "You all have fun. I'll let you know if I can join. I'll catch you later. You two lovebirds go have fun on the dance floor."

Logan frowned, but nodded. Carter replayed her words. How much could she sound like a grandma in one night? The music switched to an R&B song, and she was greeted with Barrett grinding up against Logan, while Logan moved closer to her friends to make them join in the fun. She was pretty sure she'd hurl if she had to watch Barrett paw at her all night, even more so knowing that Logan wasn't even sure she liked him.

Turning her attention back to her camera, she captured a handful of late-arriving couples and eventually set her camera down on the tripod, making sure it was out of reach of someone who'd knock it over by not paying attention. She made her way to the punch table, where Aiden was leaned up against a chair talking to a girl from his French class, named Madison.

"I'm thinking of studying prelaw," she heard him say. She smiled and busied herself, grabbing refreshments. If he was going to shoot his shot and try to talk to Madison, instead of talking *about* her like he had been for the past three years, she wasn't going to interfere.

"That's really impressive." Carter leaned out of his line of sight, so she wouldn't throw off his game. Madison was actually engaging in small talk and not brushing him off. Maybe his time to shine had come after all. Carter took a sip of the punch, and winced. It had definitely already been spiked. She looked over to where Susan, their school counselor, was happily drinking a cup and dancing to the music. Stifling a laugh, Carter ducked behind the podium and took a seat, watching it all go down. There was no way Susan could have pretended not to taste the cheap vodka, but she wasn't going to rain on their parade, and something had to be said for that level of hot mess in a counselor. Hell, she might have even seen them spike it and decided not to do a thing about it. Anything to stick it to Rumble who made her every day a living hell, no doubt.

Across from her, Alexis, who helped her write on the paper from time to time, approached her with a punch cup in her hand.

"Are you drinking the same thing I'm drinking?" she asked, her eyes widening as she smiled.

"I am," Carter said, raising her glass to cheers Alexis's. "Anything to get through the night."

"Oh, come on," Alexis said, shimmying to the music. "It's one of our last dances before the year is up, and after tonight, we're on holiday break. Come join me."

Carter weighed her options. She could sit in her seat and people watch, content to be the quiet kid in the corner. Looking over, she saw Aiden leading Madison out to the dance floor, so the option of hanging out with him was off the table. Or, she could embrace it. She looked at the punch cup and shrugged. If there was ever a time to throw caution to the wind, this might just be it. She nodded at Alexis.

"One song," she mouthed over the blaring music, as she followed Alexis out to the dance floor.

Amid the sea of her fellow classmates, she closed her eyes for a second, getting in tune with the beat. Hopefully her mother's Hispanic heritage, rhythm, and love of dancing wouldn't fail her now, even though she'd inherited more of her dad's 'white boy moves,' as he called them. She pictured her mom moving her hips to the beat the way she did no matter what song came on and channeled the energy. It might not have been the moves the hip-hop song called for, but Alexis was nodding her head.

"Yes!" Alexis screamed over the music. Carter relaxed and moved with the beat of the music.

"I was wondering when you were going to join the fun." Logan's voice in her ear made her skin tingle. She swallowed, nodded at Alexis and turned to face Logan, who dropped down low in front of her and shimmied her body up against Carter's. The movement was as confusing as it was exciting. Carter's face flushed and her heart pounded, as she looked around to make sure no one was watching. Glancing over her shoulder, she saw that Alexis had turned toward some guy she recognized from her physics class and turned her attention back toward Logan who was now facing her.

"Are you having a good night?" Logan's voice was breathless and husky from all her dancing.

"I am," she said, surprising herself with the truth in the answer. "Are you?"

"It's better now." Logan moved her shoulders as the beat sped up. "Want to grab some punch?"

For the first time in her life, Carter wanted nothing more than to stay on the dance floor, where Logan's body might brush up against hers again at any second, but it was loud.

"Yeah." Nodding her head in the direction of the table, Carter beckoned for Logan to follow.

"Sorry about earlier," Logan said, once they were away from the speakers. "He's a bit much sometimes."

"No need to apologize. I assumed you would be hanging out with your date after the dance anyway."

Logan looked over her shoulder, scanning the room. "I didn't want to," she whispered when she was sure no one could hear them. "I mean, all the stuff I said to you in confidence, I'm still figuring out. But, I did want to hang out with you."

"Where is he now?" Carter scanned the dance floor and didn't see any sight of him or his buddies.

"In the parking lot, filling up another round of flasks for the next bowl of punch." Logan rolled her eyes.

"Got to keep the party rolling, I guess," Carter said, shaking her head and laughing.

"Yeah, something like that." Logan glanced toward the table. "What do you say we grab another drink, and maybe he'll drink himself into a stupor. Then we can grab dinner after?"

"You could always just say 'no' to his invitation to go out after the dance, you know?"

Logan leaned back as if she'd never truly considered it. "We'll see," she said. "But if not, let's plan brunch tomorrow?"

It was a consolation prize, but it was better than nothing. "Deal," Carter agreed, turning toward the punch table, before she did or said something that would cross a line.

CHAPTER EIGHT

The speakers pounded, as if they'd been turned up since the party had started. Around her, Logan watched as people danced, stumbled, and made fools of themselves. *These are the moments you'll remember most.* Her dad's words played in her mind, and she was pretty sure he was right. It would be hard to wipe her memory clear of these sights.

She moved to the beat, thankful Barrett had made another trip to the parking lot. Looking around, she searched for Carter.

"What are you doing?" Josie's voice broke her concentration.

"Nothing," Logan said, quickly resuming her dance moves.

"You've been acting weird lately," Josie said, leaning closer and moving her body against Logan's.

"I haven't." Logan frowned briefly as she continued moving her body to the music. "Just been busy with Mom out of town."

"Okay," Josie said, seemingly content with the answer.

Maybe this is what people meant when they said you'd grow apart from your high school friends, only she hadn't expected it while she was still in high school. She figured the separation would come when Josie was in Oklahoma, and she was busy with her classes and practices here in Albuquerque. People did change though, and maybe she was changing too. She scanned the crowd again, locking eyes with Carter by the punch table. She smiled and nodded in Carter's direction, motioning for her to come and join them.

"Who's your new friend?" Josie asked, meeting Logan's line of sight.

"That's Carter," Logan said, turning back to face Josie. "You know her. We all have a couple of classes together."

"I know who she is, but she's never been a part of our crowd. Why now?"

"Why not?"

Josie glanced back over in the direction of the punch table. "She's coming your way," Josie said, dancing off to find the rest of their friends.

Logan scowled. Why couldn't they all dance together? If she'd figured out how cool Carter was, why couldn't anyone else embrace that? Just because she didn't play sports didn't mean Josie had to duck out of sight. She huffed and turned to try to find Carter.

"Thirsty?" Carter's voice behind her made her jump. Composing herself, she turned around and smiled. Carter held out two cups of punch and offered a bemused grin.

"Thank you." Logan accepted the drink. It was her second of the night, and she knew better than to have any more. "Last one," she said, tapping her cup against Carter's.

"For me too," Carter said, looking around. "It looks like my ride may have other plans." She nodded in Aiden's direction where he was dancing closely with a girl whose name Logan couldn't remember.

"Do you need a ride?"

"I'll Uber, or I'll have my mom pick me up." Carter shook her head, tipping back her punch cup and taking a swig. She winced at the bitter taste.

"Okay, just make sure you get home safe." Logan hated sounding like someone's mother, but sometimes people didn't make it home safe. Fear gripped her heart, and for a moment, she was taken back to the moment it had all fallen apart. Steeling her emotions, she met Carter's gaze.

"I will," Carter assured her, placing a gentle hand on her forearm. "You make sure you make it home safe too. If you need a ride, my mom would be happy to drop you off."

"What's going on here?" Barrett came up behind Logan, his voice filled with disgust. He looked from Logan to Carter and zeroed in on Carter's hand on Logan's arm. "What the hell, Logan?" He shook his head, frowning at her. "I take back the offer for buying you dinner if you're over here trying to take my girl."

"I'm not trying to take anything," Carter said, backing up. "But she's also not your property."

Logan laughed, thankful for Carter's boldness. "She's right, you know?" Logan stepped between Carter and Barrett. "But, we're just dancing. What's the big deal?"

"The look on her face is the big deal," Barrett said, bowing up his chest. "She looks like she's over here, trying to get in your pants."

"I am not," Carter said, and Logan shook her head.

"Come on, Barrett. Enough!" She looked around, thankful for the loud music, so no one else could hear what was happening. "Let's talk in the parking lot," she suggested.

"Oh you want me and her to take this outside?" he asked, looking over at Carter. "I wouldn't hit a girl."

"And that's commendable, I guess," Logan said, shaking her head. "That's not what I'm asking though. I want to talk to you outside."

"Are you okay?" Carter mouthed.

"Go outside," Logan instructed carefully to Barrett. "I'll meet you there."

Deflated, Barrett dropped his shoulders and turned toward the door.

"Don't leave without me, please," Logan asked Carter, keeping her voice low. "I might need that ride after all."

Before Carter could say anything that might either embolden her or take the wind from her sails, Logan strode out the gym, following closely behind Barrett.

He leaned up against his truck and turned to face her. "What's going on with you?"

"Nothing is going on with me," Logan said, putting her hands on her hips. "What's going on with you? You're in there, acting like a barbarian, like I'm not allowed to dance with another person."

"News flash, Logan. She likes girls." Barrett stuck his hands in his pockets, pacing. "Why do you think she's so interested in hanging out with you all the time now?"

"I'd hardly call it all of the time," Logan said, shaking her head. "We've hung out twice. First on the car ride to the game and then tonight. You weren't able to take me, remember? I had to get a ride with her."

"I had practice, and you know it. Otherwise, I would have been there to save the day. But, damn, get a lesbian with a car, and suddenly you're all over her?"

"I *wasn't* all over her. We were dancing. You were fine with me dancing with Marco tonight, but not with her. That sounds like some fragile masculinity if I've ever heard of it."

"Cut that shit out."

"Excuse me?" Logan backed up and shook her head. Crossing her arms over her chest, she let out a sad laugh. "I'm standing up for myself, when the guy who's called himself my boyfriend for three years is acting like a complete tool. What was with that display of kissing all over me in there?"

"I thought you'd like it. Hell, I thought you liked me."

"Yeah, so did I." Logan looked up to the night sky, thinking that for a brief second, maybe the beauty of the stars would bring some peace back into the night. But, in an instant Barrett was in front of her.

His lips were on hers, and she pushed him away. "Don't."

"Why?"

"I don't owe you a reason."

"It's been three years, Logan. You won't so much as touch me. You don't kiss me unless I kiss you first. Even then, you pull away. You flat out refuse to do anything more beyond kissing, even though I've done everything possible to let you know I love you."

"Wow." She wrapped her arms around her body, shivering from the cold night air. She took a couple of steps backward. "I don't owe you anything. We're done here."

"Just like that?"

"Just like that," she said. She turned to leave, but stopped. Turning back once more, she stared at him. "Give me your keys."

"Oh, so you're going to dump me and take my keys?"

"Yeah." She nodded, reaching out her hand. "I am. I'm not taking no for an answer. You should know what it means to me."

"Fine," he said, reaching in his pockets and hurling his keys to the ground. "Take whatever you want."

As he turned to walk away, she walked over to pick up his keys and headed inside. Leaning up against the doorway, she took a deep breath. No more kisses that just didn't feel right. No more waiting for him to disappear with his friends just so she could hang out with her own. No more requests to touch her body. It was finished. She straightened her shoulders and walked back to the dance floor with her head held high. First things first, she found Barrett's best friend, Marco.

"Barrett's drunk. Don't give these back to him," she said, handing the keys to Marco.

"Why don't you hold on to them?"

"Not my problem anymore." She turned to leave.

Josie grabbed her arm. "What do you mean, not your problem anymore?"

"I mean exactly what I said. He's someone else's responsibility now."

"Are you…" Josie looked her up and down. "Are you okay? Are you upset? Do you want to go to my house? I'll blow off the after-party."

"Hey," Marco said, frowning.

"I'm not going to ruin the fun of your budding relationship," Logan insisted, smiling at Marco. "Besides, I'm really fine. I promise."

"We'll get a pint of Ben and Jerry's and cry to a chick flick or some sad songs," Josie offered.

Logan laughed. "No need. I promise. I ended it, but don't tell him I said that. He's welcome to spin it how he wants." She looked around the dance floor. She didn't want to hurt him, even if he could be an insensitive prick. "In fact, don't tell anyone anything. Let them find out however it plays out. But as for me, I'm going to head home."

"Do you need a ride?" The look in Josie's eyes was pleading for more information, but Logan didn't know what to tell her. It, the spark or whatever it was, just wasn't there, and she was sick of him acting like he owned her every move. That would all come out later, whenever Marco wasn't standing right there.

"I'm good, thank you," she said, leaning in to hug Josie. "I'll fill you in on everything tomorrow, but have fun tonight," she whispered. When she thought Josie might protest again, she pulled both Marco and Josie into a hug and pushed them together as she walked away. "Go dance, be young, be crazy," she called out, as she headed toward the punch table.

"Are you okay?" Carter asked, as she approached.

"I think I'm better than okay," she said, her smile growing as she took it all in. For the first time in years, she was single. "I feel free." The admission came as a shock to her, but she motioned to the water cups beside the punch bowl. "I could use one of those. And then should we walk to grab some food and call your mom?"

Carter looked over Logan's shoulder. "He's not coming back, is he?"

Logan glanced to the doorway and shook her head. "I think his pride is damaged enough for one night. If I know him, he'll sulk for the night and maybe tomorrow. By Sunday, he'll be at my door with flowers, and I'll have to tell him to leave."

"Wow, okay," Carter said. "If you're sure, then that sounds like a plan to me."

Logan walked over, smiling at Susan as she grabbed two water cups. Logan couldn't help but laugh, noting how her lipstick was now smeared and she was dancing like she was back in the eighties.

"Too much punch for some," Logan said quietly as they stepped out of earshot.

"Too much punch for many," Carter corrected, holding her hand out to the dance floor that had now turned into nothing more than a bump-and-grind club scene.

"Tell me you got some of this on camera," Logan said, laughing as she watched the scene unfold.

"I got most of it," Carter said, joining in her laughter. "Maybe you can review the footage with me when I go to print them."

Logan glanced at the floor. Was Barrett right? Was Carter only friendly because she liked her? She looked back at Carter and relaxed her shoulders seeing Carter's hopeful smile.

"I'd like that," she said. Gripping her cup, she downed it in one swallow. "Want to get out of here?"

Whatever the reasons, she didn't have to know. She felt safe and happy, and that was what mattered most. The rest would sort itself out.

CHAPTER NINE

The night air was cold, but the stars shone brightly. Carter pulled her coat around her waist, thankful for the small outdoor heaters on the patio of the restaurant Logan had chosen. Surrounded by old gas pumps, relics of the 1940s, and the Nob Hill scenery, she smiled. This was the charm and culture she wasn't quite ready to let go of after high school. A stop along the historic Route 66, the diner had turned into a brewpub and restaurant that was every bit as lively as it was scenic.

On the outdoor speakers, contemporary radio played, and Logan swayed to the music, still feeling either the effects of the alcohol or the high of breaking up with Barrett.

"What are you getting?" Logan asked, glancing up from the menu.

"I'm thinking the burger with extra chile and a side of cheese fries to split."

"So you're not a vegan?"

Carter laughed and shook her head. "Did you think I was?"

"I think someone said it once," Logan said, shaking her head. "Sorry, I think that's a stereotype."

"There are a lot of those." Carter nodded, glancing down at the menu. "But don't sweat it. I eat meat. What are you getting?"

"Cheese fries do sound good," Logan said, biting her lip as she perused the choices in front of her. "I'm thinking a Philly."

"Good choice."

After the waitress came and took their orders, Carter leaned her forearms on the table. "So how are you holding up?"

"I should have done that years ago, honestly," she said, looking up at the sky. "I kind of feel bad that I didn't, but I am just figuring it all out. I didn't think I didn't like him until I knew I didn't."

"What changed?" Carter wanted to keep the conversation light, but she also wanted to make sure Logan was okay. Breaking up with someone after years of dating had to take a toll.

"Our conversation the other day really opened up my eyes, I guess." Logan pulled her jacket tighter.

"Do you want this seat? It's closer to the heater." Carter stood and gestured to her chair.

"No. Thank you though. You're so nice." Logan's eyes clouded, and she shook her head.

Carter wanted to press, but the waitress showed up with their waters. As she walked away, Carter leveled her gaze.

"What's going on? You can talk to me."

Logan took a deep breath and took a sip of her water. "If I don't ask now when I have a bit of liquid courage, I'm not sure I ever will. Barrett said something tonight, and I think he's just an ass, but it made me think."

"What did he say?"

Carter braced herself as Logan stared into her eyes. "He said you're only nice to me because you like me."

The accusation hung in the air, and Carter weighed her options. She didn't want to lie. She took a sip of her water, buying a second.

"I'm sorry," Logan said, shaking her head "That's ridiculous. I know."

"It's not ridiculous." Carter cleared her throat. She chose her words carefully. "I like hanging out with you. I'm a fairly nice person and would have probably been this nice to anyone who was a decent human. You're more than decent, and we enjoy a lot of the same things, so me being nice to you has nothing to do with that."

It was honest, albeit not totally. Carter *did* like Logan, as much as she wanted to fight it. Across from her, she watched as Logan's face fell.

"So you don't like me?"

"Do you want me to?" It was deflection, but she decided it was fair play if she was being put on the spot.

Logan laughed nervously. "I love the way Nob Hill looks at night."

That was also deflection, but Carter would take it. They were both still figuring out where they stood, and she was happy for a distraction. "Yeah, this is one of my favorite spots to people watch and just take it all in."

Logan opened her mouth to speak, but the waitress showed up in lightning speed, delivering their order of cheese fries.

Carter popped one into her mouth, thankful for both sustenance after a long night and for the distraction.

"What if I like girls?" The question rang out abruptly.

Carter choked on her fry and stared at Logan across the table. Taking a long drink of her water, she tried to clear her throat. "What?" she croaked after a minute.

"I mean, what if the reason I'm not into Barrett is that I like girls?"

"Do you like girls?"

"I don't know." Logan shoved a cheese fry into her mouth and chewed furiously. "You're supposed to be the expert."

"Hardly an expert." Carter's heart threatened to beat out of her chest as she stared at Logan. "Maybe you just didn't like him, but you like other guys, right?"

Logan shrugged. "Maybe, but which guys are those?"

Carter grabbed her fork and picked through her fries. She didn't want to dismiss Logan, but she'd also had a couple of drinks, so Carter wasn't sure how much of this to take at face value.

"What type of people are you attracted to?"

Logan looked out across the street toward a bar with a rooftop lounge. She smiled at the dancing bodies and shook her head. "That's the thing, I'm not sure. But what if I've just never explored the possibilities?"

"What possibilities are those?" Carter gripped her napkin, hoping it would stop her hands from shaking. Maybe Aiden had been right all along. Maybe Logan liked her too. The *possibilities*, as Logan called them, were endless. She swallowed hard, pushing aside the pang of hope. She was being presumptuous.

"Possibilities that maybe I'm not broken, that maybe I just haven't looked where my heart wants to go."

"Where's that?"

The waitress popped back up with two towering plates of food, interrupting with the quickest service ever. Carter quickly thanked her and fought the urge to stuff her face with a burger. "What are you saying, Logan?"

"I don't want to date another boy," Logan said quietly, before taking a huge bite of her sandwich.

"That's totally fine," Carter said, following suit and stuffing her mouth, so she couldn't talk.

Across from her, Logan reached for a napkin and wiped her mouth. She swallowed and grinned. "If I'm going to date girls, should I be more ladylike than this, or is cheese on my face okay?"

Carter laughed, thankful for a moment of levity. "Cheese on your face is fine, I think. I mean, who am I to say? I've never really dated anyone, remember?"

"Right." Logan nodded. "But you don't hate the cheese on the face?"

"I don't hate it," Carter said, shaking her head. It would be impossible to hate the cute smile on Logan's face, as she beamed ear to ear with cheese dripping from her lip and a giant sandwich in her hand. It created the perfect contrast against her formal dress and tailored peacoat.

"Is your mom really going to be cool picking us up this late?" Logan glanced at her phone.

"It's only ten thirty. She'll be fine. Besides, she's always said that I can call no questions asked, any time. What about you?" Carter picked up her burger. "Will your parents be upset?"

"No." Logan shook her head. "My dad is expecting me to sleep at Josie's, but he won't question it if I come home." Logan started to take a bite but stopped. "Thanks for another ride, by the way. One of these days, I'll figure out my transportation issues."

"Don't sweat it," Carter said. Logan's eyes darkened, and Carter's heart fell. She wished Logan didn't have to face ghosts every day. "I'm really sorry about what happened."

"I really miss him," Logan said, swallowing hard. Carter wanted to speak words of comfort, but sat in the silence and waited. "A big brother is someone you just never expect to lose. After the crash, I just couldn't drive again. I never wanted to get back behind the wheel."

"That's understandable," Carter said, reaching across the table to place her hand on Logan's. "Take your time and heal, and there's always public transportation or a friend with a car. Don't put a timeline on yourself."

Logan smiled, wrapping her fingers around Carter's. "Thank you." She looked up to make eye contact. "I appreciate it."

"Of course." Carter was careful not to pull her hand away from Logan's. She liked the way it felt there. Protective. Safe. Comforting. Intimate. "Grief doesn't have a timeline. The human heart is a strange beast."

"That it is." Logan nodded and grabbed her sandwich with her free hand and took a bite. As they finished up the meal in silence, Carter took in every second. The way the light reflected off Logan's smile, the way Logan's hand felt in her own, the softness of Logan's blue eyes, the ease in which they could just exist.

She was falling, only this time for a maybe not-so-straight girl. Her heart leapt at the thought, but she worked to keep her emotions at bay. Falling too hard too fast, especially while Logan was still figuring things out, could only end in disaster.

"I wish we were older," Logan said, breaking the silence after the waitress took their plates and brought the bill.

"Why's that?"

Logan glanced back to the rooftop bar. "I'd love to go sit up there until the sun came up and learn everything there is to know about you."

Carter followed her gaze and joined the daydream. How wonderful would that be? She thought about inviting Logan to hang out at her house after dinner, but figured that would come across too forward. She wasn't looking for anything like that, but she didn't want the night to end either.

"That would be nice," she finally said, looking back toward Logan. "But, for now, how about we head home and plan to hang out again soon?"

"Works for me," Logan said, standing from her seat.

Carter shot a quick text to her mom and stood, walking around the table to join Logan. She thought about looping her arm around Logan, but paused. Was it too much too soon? Would that cross a line? Brushing the thoughts aside, she walked side by side with Logan to the exit.

"So have you still not been on a date?" Logan asked, looking at Carter with a smile.

"I'd say this doesn't count as a date just yet." She tilted her head to the side. "Do you want to go on a date with me?"

"I thought you'd never ask."

Carter's heart pounded, and her entire body tingled at the sight of Logan's smile. She wanted nothing more than to grab Logan and kiss her, but she resisted the urge. There was a better time and place for this. Late night, after some alcohol and a school dance just meant that there was pressure. There wasn't clear thinking. Logan could wake up tomorrow and regret the whole thing.

"Wednesday night?" Carter decided to seize the moment and go for it.

"Wednesday night works for me," Logan said, bringing her arms up to pull Carter in for a hug. "Where are we going?"

On Wednesday, her mom would be working late, presenting to her college class. "I'll cook. I'll text you the address."

"A home-cooked meal for a first date?" Logan raised an eyebrow and nodded. "I'll be there."

"Maybe we can catch a movie or a show at the Sunset Theater, if there's anyone playing after?"

"Dinner and a show? You're scoring points already, Carter."

Carter opened her mouth to speak, but her mom pulled up right as she was going to respond. "After you," she said, opening up the back door of the car.

Once they'd dropped Logan off at her house, her mom turned to her with a raised eyebrow. "Want to tell me about your friend?"

"There's nothing to tell, Mom," Carter said, smiling as she leaned back into her seat. *Yet*, she added silently.

CHAPTER TEN

Christmas music played through the speakers of her dad's prized possession, his restored turntable. Beside Logan, her dad hummed along to "The Little Drummer Boy," while Ben dug through the box of ornaments.

"Look at your handiwork," Ben said, laughing as he held up a snowman she'd fashioned out of toilet paper that her mom had held on to for some ungodly reason.

"Me?" Logan shot back. "Have you seen your handprint turkey that you made for the tree? Classic and wrong holiday, all in one."

"Priceless works of art," her dad said, laughing as he strung the lights.

Ben's face darkened, but only briefly, and Logan turned away from him. She knew he'd stumbled into the section of the box that contained Luke's artwork and ornaments. Usually Mom sorted through, so they were spared the struggle of remembering the loss of their brother at such a joyous time. Not that it mattered, they all knew he should still be here, and his failed art attempts were no laughing matter. Now they were exactly as her father had said, priceless works of art. She swallowed and put a smile on her face. Walking over to Ben, she put her arm around his shoulder.

"Let's leave the crafts off for this year." She turned to her dad. "What do you say?"

"I'm leaning on you for direction here," her dad said with a goofy grin. "Your mom usually calls the shots, so you can be in charge if you'd like." He reached into a box beside him and pulled out an elf hat. Placing it on her head, he beamed. "Head elf, tag in at anytime."

"I'm capturing this for sure," Ben said, pulling out his phone and snapping a picture before Logan could protest. "Priceless family memories and blackmail, should I ever need it," he added with a smirk. Putting his phone back in his pocket, he stood and joined them in front of the tree.

After putting the final touches on the décor, they stepped back, admiring their work. Her dad pulled out his phone. "Looks like we finished just in time," he said, wrapping the two of them into a warm embrace. "I have to head into the office." He tallied off some time on his hand, and looked from Ben to Logan. "Do you want to do dinner tonight? We could go out."

"I have plans tonight, or I would," Logan said, her own phone buzzing in her pocket, reminding her she'd blown Josie off for long enough that she'd be getting an interrogation this evening.

"Same, actually," Ben said, his smile growing.

"Benjamin with plans?" Logan said, dropping her jaw open in faux shock. "Care to share with the class?"

"You first," Ben said, narrowing his gaze at Logan.

"Dinner with Josie. You?"

"A date with Adriana," he said, straightening his shoulders. "I won't be out late," he added, turning his attention to their dad.

"You two have fun. I'll pick up something on the way home, and hopefully I'll get tomorrow to hang around here, if you're around."

"Maybe we can go hike in the Sandias, or something," Logan offered.

"I'll dig out my boots," her dad said, kissing the top of her head. He gathered his briefcase, before heading for the door.

"A date, huh?" Logan asked when the front door had closed behind him. "Where are you taking her?"

Ben shifted his weight, the air of confidence he'd displayed only seconds before now gone. "I was thinking pizza and the River of Lights at the BioPark." He shrugged. "Is that lame?"

"What girl wouldn't want to go for pizza? And then top that off with the annual holiday light show that's as romantic as it is fun, no matter how old you get. That's perfect, Ben."

"Really? I want to impress her."

She laughed and resisted the urge to mimic her mom in saying *what girl wouldn't be impressed by you?* In all fairness, though, he was the kindest-hearted boy she'd ever met. "She'll be impressed. No doubt."

"Thanks," he said, nodding and taking a deep breath.

"Just don't overdo it on the cologne," Logan instructed, turning and heading for the stairs.

"Got it." She laughed at the serious tone of his voice.

"Is it true, by the way?" Ben called out behind her.

"Is what true?" She looked over her shoulder to see Ben looking at his phone.

"Did you and Barrett break up? I didn't want to put you on the spot in front of Dad"—he paused and looked her in the eye—"unlike some people."

"Sorry about that. I figured Mr. Share-It-All wouldn't mind giving us the details of his date."

He moved his head side to side. "I really don't mind, I guess, but you're dodging the question."

"Touché. We did."

"Are you okay? Do you need anything?" He took a couple of steps toward her and stopped.

"I'm fine," she said, holding her hands up in the air to stop the undeniably sweet, but unnecessary, display of little brother protectiveness. "I broke up with him, but keep that between me and you. I don't know how it'll all play out, but you already know how high school drama goes. I really don't care what he says or how it goes down, but I'm happy to be done with it."

"Wow," Ben said, nodding. "I kind of always thought you two were going to do the happily ever after thing, where you got married, had two kids, and bought a house and all that."

"That was never in the cards." The words came easily and rang with truth. She crinkled her nose. "I don't know what the happily ever after looks like, but it's not with him." She thought back to the previous night, the way Carter had looked at her with such awe and such intimacy. She looked down to the floor and then back to Ben. She stared at him for a minute, wishing she had the guts to spill her life as easily as he did. It would have been so good to talk it through with someone she knew wouldn't judge, but would just listen. Instead, she smiled. "I'm going to go get ready, but good luck tonight. I hope you have fun."

"Thanks," he said, turning back toward the kitchen. "You too!"

In her room, she changed out of the Christmas pajamas she'd been wearing to add to the festivities. She glanced at the clock and then to her bedside table.

She walked over, picking up the photo of Luke and Ben with their arms around her. It had been taken on one of their final outings, a family hike and picnic in Jemez Springs. Running her fingers around the edge of the frame, she took a seat on the edge of the bed. She leaned back against her pillow and let the tears fall for the first time in a while.

Closing her eyes, she could see it all so clearly. He'd been tired after practice and asked her to drive home instead, something she'd done a number of times successfully. She gripped the frame tighter, reminding herself that it wasn't her fault. No one could have seen the truck barreling through a red light. She relived it all again, the crash, the broken glass, the screams. Her body shuddered, as she placed the frame back in its place. She could see it all so clearly, but somehow in the aftermath, all she'd been left with were memories of the big brother she'd loved, crippling fear, unresolved trauma, and a shoulder injury that wouldn't go away.

"I miss you," she said, giving the photo a final glance. "I wish you were here. Maybe you'd be able to talk some sense into me."

Despite her tears, she smiled, remembering how he always approached life in such a happy-go-lucky way, much like Ben, but with even more of a free spirit. He would have told her to go with the flow, that she didn't have to have it all figured out. She gave the photo a sad smile. He wouldn't have wanted her to hide from things, just because they might be unpleasant.

Pulling out her phone, she took a deep breath, hit the button to call her mom, and waited as the phone rang.

"Logan?" Her mom's voice was filled with surprise, and she silently chided herself for waiting so long to make the call.

"Hey, Mom," Logan said, her voice hoarse.

"Have you been crying? Are you okay?" Even though they were miles apart, Logan could just imagine the crease in her forehead deepening.

"I'm fine, Mom," she said, clearing her throat. "I just miss you. How's Grandma?"

"She's hanging in there." There was a muffled noise in the background and some shuffling. "I'm in the hallway now," her mom said. "She's sleeping, so I didn't want to disturb her. I'm so glad you called. Fill me in on everything I've missed."

Logan wished she could pull her in for a hug, and just have her close by, but she resisted the urge to ask when she was coming home. The story was still the same. None of them knew for sure. She regaled her mom with tales of the game and the dance, leaving out the part about the breakup and her after-party with Carter. Those details could come later, when she understood more of what she was feeling.

"I've missed so much." Her mother's voice held hints of sadness, and Logan's heart fell. She hadn't wanted to make her sad.

"It's okay, Mom. There will be plenty left for you to catch up on when you get back."

"Tacos and girls' night as soon as I'm home?"

Logan smiled. "I wouldn't miss it for the world."

By the time she hung up the phone, she felt a little lighter, as if she'd somehow made some progress in the whole growing up process. She bit her lip and cupped her phone in her hand. There was no way she was going to have it all figured out overnight, but she might as well stop running from things that made her uncomfortable.

Want to come over? She typed out the text to Josie and hit Send. Within seconds, Josie replied.

On my way.

She looked over to her bulletin board, covered in pictures of her with Josie in every imaginable activity from the time they were ten. There was no reason to feel nervous, but her heart raced. It felt as if her entire world had been turned upside down in a matter of weeks, and it was no wonder Josie kept pressuring her to figure out what was wrong. People didn't just break up with their boyfriend of three years on a whim, disappear from their friends, and reinvent themselves. Or did they? She bit the inside of her cheek and walked over to the board. Focusing on the picture they'd taken on a summer vacation to Padre Island, Texas, the year before, her heart settled into a normal rhythm. On that trip they'd promised that whatever life threw at them, they'd find their way to the other side. And, just like with Ben, there was no need to over-share details until she had a better grasp on things.

Before she could dwell on her thoughts more, Josie bounded into her room. She jumped as the door swung open.

"What's up?" Josie asked, hopping onto Logan's bed. "Where'd you disappear to last night?"

"I didn't disappear," Logan said, taking a spot opposite of Josie. "I just found another ride home."

"With Carter?" Josie propped herself up on the overstuffed basketball pillow that had been on Logan's bed since she was twelve. It was a relic of childhood she probably should have gotten rid of, but she just couldn't bring herself to do it yet.

"Yeah, her mom gave me a ride home. You two should hang out sometime. She's pretty cool."

"I'll take your word for it," Josie said, looking around the room as if she hadn't been in it hundreds of times. "What's your new fascination with her?"

"It's not a fascination. People are allowed to make new friends."

"They are." Josie cocked her head to the side. "They just don't normally do so in the middle of senior year, especially with someone they've never talked to before."

"I don't think it's all that weird." She looked into Josie's eyes and studied her for a minute. What was it she wasn't saying? Did she think the same things as Barrett? "Tell me about your night," she said, changing the subject. "Did you and Marco go to Frontier with everyone, or did you have a *private* after-party?" She raised her eyebrows suggestively, laughing at the way Josie's mouth fell open.

"Why not both?"

"Did you?" Logan leaned in closer. She might not have a sex life to talk about, but she was intensely curious on living vicariously through her best friend.

Josie smiled and glanced to the floor, as if contemplating her response.

"Come on," Logan said, propping herself up on her elbows. "It's me. Spill."

"The night just felt so perfect." Josie looked up at the ceiling. "Not just the dance. That sounds too cliché, but we laughed and danced and then went to eat with everyone. After that, he drove me out to look at the stars, and I just felt it, so we went for it."

"And?"

"And"—Josie rolled over to face Logan again—"I don't know. It wasn't magical like you hear about. It wasn't mind-blowing, but it just felt right. I don't know how to explain it."

"Are you glad you did it?" Logan watched as Josie's face lit up, and she smiled. Logan looked up at the ceiling, wondering what it would be like to feel that same excitement at a touch.

"I am," she said after a moment. "Like I said, it just felt right, and I'm sure it'll be better next time."

"Was it bad?" Logan crinkled her nose.

"No, it wasn't bad. It just was kind of a learning experience, I guess. Remember how it was when we were first learning anything, and we kind of fumbled around with it? It was like that. It was a new experience. It was something I really wanted to do though, so I'm happy I did." Josie paused, looking her up and down. "Enough about me. Tell me what happened with you and Barrett."

"Your story is way more entertaining." Logan laughed. "You can't really compare an anti-climatic breakup with having sex for the first time."

"Still, I want to know the details. I shared. Now it's your turn." Josie reached over, snagging the bottle of water by Logan's bed and taking a drink.

Logan smiled at the move. Josie was right. They shared everything, even drinks. "I just wasn't feeling it anymore." She looked around the room, noting the pictures she'd have to take down, showing Barrett with his possessive arms around her all over the room.

"What do you mean?"

"Whatever 'it' is," she said, using air quotes to get her point across, "it just wasn't there."

"The spark?" Josie grinned. "Is that why you never really wanted to kiss him or do anything with him?"

Logan blushed and covered her face with a pillow. The topic had come up time and time again, and now that Josie had decided to sleep with the guy she liked just a short time into dating, it only added to the anomaly of her not wanting to. "I guess," she said after a minute. "You said it just felt right with Marco. It never felt like that with Barrett."

"Never?" Josie leaned back and furrowed her brow. "Not even in the beginning?"

Logan shook her head.

"When you were making out, you never thought, 'oh my god, I'm going to lose control'? Not even once?"

Was she saying too much? She bit her lip, and shook her head.

"Damn," Josie said, letting out a sigh. "You do deserve better then. Is he a bad kisser?"

"How would I know? He's the only person I've kissed."

"Well, he must not be great." Josie shook her head. "Don't worry, I won't say anything. I know you're taking the high road here and everything, but I hope you find much better than that next time." She stretched her back and leaned closer. "You deserve to feel all the insanity of teenage hormones." She rolled over onto her back and giggled. "Trust me."

"Okay, so it *was* good," Logan teased.

"It was, and I'm really excited to do it again."

"I'm happy for you," Logan said, sitting up on the bed. "One day, I'll find that too."

"Are you going to wait for college, or are you looking to rebound?"

Logan laughed and shook her head. "I'm not making any plans," she said. Her mouth went dry. She'd already started making plans. Wednesday, she had a date. She looked down at the floor, unable to look Josie in the eye and lie.

"What's going on?" Josie stood and walked toward Logan's side of the bed. "What aren't you saying?"

"I think I'm just going to focus on figuring out what I want for a while."

"There's nothing wrong with that," Josie said, eyeing her carefully. "If you want to make a list, I'm here for it. Instead of going out, we can order in and stay up talking about what it is you want in a man. Maybe it's someone at school, or maybe it's some college guy you haven't even met yet."

Maybe it's a girl I already have. The thought shot around her head like the ball in the vintage pinball machine at the old diner down the street.

"Here," Josie said, pulling out a notebook from Logan's backpack and grabbing a pen from the bedside table. "I'm ready. Just start listing some things."

She wasn't going to take no for an answer, Logan could tell, so she turned to face Josie, sitting crisscross on the bed. Closing her eyes, she drifted back to the night before. Even if it hadn't been a date and even though she'd been on a hundred dates with Barrett over the years, it was the closest thing she'd ever *felt* to being on a date. Her eyes flew open, considering the thought. Not once had she felt that tingle when he so much as touched her arm. Even now, she craved for her hand to brush up against Carter's again.

"That look," Josie said with a nod. "Whatever you're thinking about. That's it. I want to write that down. Start talking."

Josie drew an oversized heart on the page, and Logan laughed. It all felt so childish, but she couldn't resist. "Okay, I want someone who makes me laugh." She thought back to Carter's dry wit, and the way she so easily made Logan smile. "Someone who makes me feel at ease just by being myself, even if I'm a messy eater and get cheese all over my face." Josie laughed, but wrote it down.

"What else? You want a funny guy who likes your cheese-covered face. I need more to go on."

Guy. The word hung in the air, but Logan moved past it. "Someone who is a deep thinker and challenges me to look past just the surface level of things."

"The anti-Barrett. Got it," Josie said, making a note.

Logan looked at the paper. Josie had written 'not a dumbass.' She laughed. "You have such a poetic way with words. Has anyone ever told you that?"

"Just trying to play matchmaker, ma'am," she said, tapping the pen on the notebook. "What else?" Josie's pen hovered above the page in anticipation, and Logan wanted to say so much more, but she chose her words carefully.

"I want someone who makes me feel that desire, that feeling you talked about. I want someone who believes in me and encourages me to try new things."

"Okay, so far we've got sexy, smart, and funny. What about looks?"

Logan reached for the bottle of water, buying a minute to compose her thoughts. "Dark hair. Barrett was blond, so it's probably a good idea to switch that up. A nice smile. Good sense of style." She listed off the vague attributes like she was creating a shopping list, and nodded.

"This could really be anyone," Josie said, shaking her head at the list. "I guess we might have to go out after all, and I can point out guys. Then you can tell me if they're your type or not."

Logan's stomach flip-flopped. "No, please. Let's just stay in. I think I deserve at least a night off from guys and dating to just hang out with my best friend."

"Fine," Josie said, crumpling the list in her hand. "We'll stay in, but I'm not going to let you just sit back and wait for someone to come to you."

"I don't want to search right now."

"Okay, I guess that's fine." Josie flipped through her phone. "I'm feeling Chinese takeout. You?"

"Orange chicken, extra egg rolls."

"Lo mein?"

Logan nodded, rolling onto her back. Staring up at the ceiling, she breathed a sigh of relief. She'd survived round one of the inquisition. She could skate by for a while longer, until she knew what was going on.

Beside her, her phone buzzed.

"Who's that?" Josie's eyes lit up with curiosity.

Carter's name flashed across the screen, and Logan's mouth lifted into a smile. "My mom," she said, pulling the phone in closer.

It was just a white lie, but it was safer for now. "I'll be right back," she said, taking her phone with her to the bathroom. She couldn't be on her phone all day, or Josie would be asking questions, but sneaking a text here and there wasn't a crime—especially not when Carter hit every qualifier on her list.

CHAPTER ELEVEN

Soft music played on her speakers while Carter chopped veggies. Three hours of online cooking videos, followed by a quick trip to the farmers' market and the grocery store, and six outfit changes later, she felt like she might be equipped for this. She hummed along with the music and tried to focus on the task at hand, but her hands shook as her nerves built.

Why had she offered to cook? Wouldn't it have been easier to let someone else handle the heavy lifting for a first date? She wrung her hands on the kitchen towel and pulled her phone from her apron pocket. She still had another fifteen minutes before Logan was supposed to show up. Checking the pasta on the stove, she walked to the dining room and picked up the candle her mother always kept in the center of the table. This one was leather and amber. That would set just the right ambiance. She lit it and placed the plates on the table.

Nothing easy is worth having. Her mother's words rang in her ears. A former therapist turned psychology professor at the university, her mother had always been one for feeling things deeply, trying your hardest, and going the extra mile. She took a deep breath. She'd make her mom proud, even if she hadn't been completely honest about tonight's plans. She'd only said she was having dinner with a friend, and her mom hadn't pressed for details.

With a sigh, she shoved her hands in her pockets. She didn't want to keep secrets, but she also didn't want to blow things out of proportion. Logan had been drinking before she said all those things, and even when she said them, she hadn't been sure. There was no sense in putting the cart before the horse. They'd see what tonight brought, no pressure either way.

She really didn't want to be a science experiment though. With a laugh, she thought about those volcanoes they made in elementary, how they'd explode when you put the right ingredients inside the chamber. If there were ever an accurate depiction of the type of science experiment she'd be, that was it. Pent up anxiety and overthinking streaming into the air when finally allowed to breathe.

She checked the oven, and pulled out the chicken. Dicing it on the cutting board, she busied herself, putting the final touches on the dishes.

Alfredo gnocchi with chicken and veggies wasn't exactly a showstopper, but it was freshly prepared with…she stopped herself. She couldn't even think the word 'love.' It was prepared with care, she corrected. Like clockwork, she set the garlic bread on the table, right as Logan knocked on the front door.

Wiping her sweaty palms on her pants legs, she straightened her shoulders and walked to the door.

Hello. Hi. What's up? She practiced the greetings, but they all sounded ridiculous in her head. Clearing her throat, she smiled and opened the door.

"Hey," Logan said, smiling and breaking apart the tension Carter felt.

"Come in," Carter said, motioning for Logan to step inside the entryway.

Logan held one hand behind her back and offered a sheepish grin. "I…" She shook her head. "I got you something, but I don't really know how this all works." She pulled her hand out from behind her back and presented a single long-stemmed red rose. "Is it too much? Is it cheesy?"

"It's perfect." Carter accepted the rose, bringing it to her nose and inhaling its fragrant scent. "Thank you."

Logan stepped inside the doorway and looked around the room.

"Here, want me to take your coat?" Carter offered.

"Sure, thank you." Logan slipped out of the dark brown leather jacket, revealing her deep red top.

Red was, indeed, her color. Carter tore her eyes away, hanging the jacket on the rack and motioning to the table. "I hope you're hungry. Dinner is served."

"You made this?" Logan's eyes widened at the spread on the table.

Garlic bread, bowls of salad and pasta at each of their places.

"I did," Carter said, taking a seat across from the place she'd set for Logan.

"Wow, where'd you learn to cook?"

"My mom taught me when I was younger. We had a lot of time just the two of us, and she works a lot of nights." Carter took a sip from her water glass. "But honestly, I pulled this recipe from the Internet."

"No shame in that," Logan said with a laugh. Grabbing a piece of the bread, she dipped it into the garlic and basil oil Carter had placed in the center of the table. "I don't really cook. There was never a ton of time to learn between practices, homework, and all of that. We eat a lot of takeout at home. This is like a feast."

Carter smiled, watching Logan taste the bread with a head nod. "This is delicious," she said, after swallowing. "Thank you for dinner."

"You're very welcome."

Logan bit her lip, and her eyes sparkled with something she wasn't saying. Carter took a bite of her food, intent not to read too much into the gesture.

"How's your break been so far?" Carter asked between bites.

Logan stopped the salad fork on the way to her mouth and looked across the table. "It's been good, kind of weird, but not bad. You?"

"Mine has been uneventful." She reached for her napkin, placing it in her lap. "Why has it been weird?"

Logan took a bite of salad, chewing while she moved her shoulders back and forth as though she was thinking of a right answer. Carter looked down at the table. Maybe she shouldn't have asked. She didn't really want to hear about Barrett again, although she'd stomach it if Logan needed an outlet. Damn her mother's never-ending psychology lessons. They'd made her a good listener, maybe too good.

Logan swallowed and took a drink of water. "My mom's still out of town, so my dad's been trying really hard to do all the holiday things," she said, finally. "And other than that, Josie has been really pressuring me to start dating again." She looked down at the floor. "I've been avoiding going into too many details with her, just for now. Is that okay?" Darkness clouded her eyes, and Carter reached across the table, placing a gentle hand on Logan's arm.

"It's fine to go at your own pace. I didn't tell my mom, if that makes you feel any better."

"Oh god," Logan said with a cringe. "Your mom. I didn't say or do anything stupid in front of her that would make her suspect we're on a date tonight, did I?"

Carter laughed and shook her head. "My mom would think any girl I ever looked at was a potential girlfriend." She closed her mouth quickly, wishing she could recant the word. Logan didn't seem bothered by it, so she pressed forward. "She's always overly interested in my dating life, or lack thereof, but you didn't do anything wrong." She looked at her plate, and moved a piece of romaine over to the side. "Do you remember everything you said?"

Her fears that it had all been an in-the-moment confession, clouded by alcohol and not steeped in truth, came back front and center.

"I remember." Logan nodded. "I wasn't drunk. I'd just had a couple of drinks. I'm sorry if it was a lot to take in all at once."

"No need to apologize," Carter said, grabbing a forkful of pasta and trying the dish for the first time. The mix of flavors exploded in her mouth, making her glad she'd decided to go for a home-cooked meal.

"This is incredible." Logan echoed her thoughts, wiping her mouth with her napkin.

"It really is," Carter said, no longer looking at the pasta but across the table at Logan.

Logan grinned, her dimple showing as she diverted her eyes for a second. "I like you," she blurted out, before casting her eyes back toward the pasta and shoving a large bite into her mouth.

"Good. I like you too." The admission was simple, but held enough weight to make Carter's heart swell.

As they finished up dinner and talked about Christmas plans, Carter stared at the single rose in the middle of the table. It was something she'd cherish—the first gift given to her on her first real date.

"Do you want some help with the dishes?" Logan asked as she gathered her empty plate. "That's really my only specialty in the kitchen."

"You wash, I'll dry," Carter said.

"Teamwork makes the dream work." As soon as she spoke the words, she shook her head. "Maybe by date number two, I'll settle in and not be as awkward."

At the mention of a second date, Carter smiled. She was doing something right to have scored not only one, but two dates with Logan. "Awkward looks kind of cute on you," she said, laughing as she stood and gathered the remaining plates.

As they washed and dried, Carter tried to sort through her feelings. This type of domesticity was something she'd imagined for years down the road, not here in her mother's house and certainly not with Logan.

"What's next on the agenda?" Logan asked, reaching for the dishtowel in Carter's hands. For a moment, it looked like she might lean in for a kiss, but she pulled back, wiping her hands dry.

Carter cleared her throat and shoved her hands in her pockets. "That depends on what you'd like to do."

Logan's eyebrow shot up in question.

"We can go to the movies." She paused and tilted her head to the side. "I really don't even know what kind of movies you're into, but we can check show times online. Or we could go check out a band downtown. Or…" She looked down to the floor and considered throwing out the third option all together so there wouldn't be any weird pressure.

"Or what?" Logan asked.

"Or we could get into the Christmas spirit and watch a sappy holiday movie on TV here. Your call."

"I like rom-coms, action movies, and comedies," Logan said, reaching out to take Carter's hand. Logan's eyes darted to where their fingers now intertwined, and Carter thought she might pull back again, but she stayed. "Just since you didn't know. I figured that might be important info for later."

"Noted." Carter nodded. "So what do you think?"

"I could go for a little Christmas spirit, I think." Logan looked up at the ceiling, then back to Carter. She nodded decisively. "Yeah, that would be nice. With my mom out of town, everything has been weird. We'd have normally watched a handful of Christmas movies by now, so I think that sounds nice." She shook her head. "Not that I want to hang out with you like I'd hang out with my mom. Maybe the concert?"

"Awkward does look really cute on you," Carter said, laughing as she squeezed Logan's hand. "Let's stay in. If you get hungry later, I picked up some popcorn and movie snacks, just in case."

"You really thought of everything." Logan's eyes sparkled as she looked into Carter's, and Carter smiled. Logan took a deep breath and leaned forward. For a second, Carter's heart stopped. She held her breath as Logan's lips came closer. Her stomach tightened. She could smell the floral scent from Logan's perfume. At the last second, Logan moved to the side, kissing Carter's cheek instead of her lips.

"Is the TV in the living room?" Logan asked, pulling away, breathless. "I mean, of course it's in the living room, right? That's where televisions go." She laughed and shrugged. "Shall we head that way?"

Feeling every bit as flustered as Logan looked, Carter nodded. Never letting go of Logan's hand, she grabbed a couple of sodas from the fridge and led the way.

"Here you go," Carter said, grandly gesturing to the couch. She handed Logan a soda and turned around to catch her breath. She grabbed the remote and took a seat close to Logan, but not so close as to be touching. She was sure, if they were too close, she wouldn't be able to focus on anything. "Hallmark, Lifetime, Netflix, one of the classics, something new?"

"Let's find a new one," Logan suggested. Carter flipped through the menu, reading descriptions. When Logan put her hand on Carter's knee, she tensed. Resisting the urge to toss the remote onto a far cushion and turn her attention to Logan fully, she swallowed hard. "How about this one?" she asked, pointing to the TV with her free hand. "Looks like it's the perfect blend of sappy and funny."

"That sounds good," Logan said, her voice suddenly deeper than it had been before.

Carter selected the show and glanced to Logan out of the corner of her eye. Logan's attention wasn't on the TV either. Instead, she was staring at Carter with a smile Carter hadn't seen on her before. Seductive was the word that came to mind. She straightened her shoulders, before leaning back into the cushion.

Carter's mind raced with possibilities, but she worked to slow her breathing. She didn't want to move too fast. She *wanted* to, but with Logan, there was more at stake. Not only was Logan just testing the waters, it was Carter's first time actually getting to date someone she liked. She took a deep breath, and placed her hand on top of Logan's. This was nice and PG-rated.

The opening music started on the screen, but Carter no longer cared about whether or not the city girl visiting her family in the country found true love or not. Logan's fingers ran up and down her hand, sending waves of desire up her spine. She shifted in her seat, turning her attention to Logan.

"Are we playing with fire?" she asked, opting for the honest approach.

Logan flashed her a playful grin. "I'd like to say I don't know what you mean, but..." She trailed off, glancing to the screen before turning back to stare into Carter's eyes. "All I know is, I have never wanted to kiss anyone so badly." Logan bit her lip and let out a long exhale.

Carter's heart pounded. Her eyes trailed to Logan's lips, those soft lips that had left such a sweet touch on her cheek just moments earlier. "That makes two of us," she managed.

"You did select a movie with mistletoe in the title, you know? If we need an excuse to go ahead and give in, I think that might suffice."

"Are you sure you're ready?"

"I'm more than sure," Logan said, sitting taller in her seat. Leaning over, she brought her face inches from Carter's and raised an eyebrow. Carter nodded, and Logan's lips crashed into her own. As sleigh bells rang on the TV, Logan's tongue massaged Carter's bottom lip, and she let out a soft sigh. Tangling her hand in Logan's hair, she deepened the kiss. After a moment, she pulled back, and took a steadying breath.

"It was everything you said it would be," Logan said, her voice thick. "It was all of that and more." She leaned in for another quick kiss, before pulling herself back into her seat.

Carter wanted more, so much more, but she nestled her head under Logan's arm, in her heart knowing it was exactly as Logan had said. It was every bit as intimate, soft, and full of passion as any kiss she'd ever had, and she'd happily wait for more.

CHAPTER TWELVE

The sound of clanking weights clamored around him, and Barrett pushed through his last two reps on the bench press machine. His adrenaline running high, he hopped off the bench and let out a rally cry.

"Nice work today, man," Marco said, coming up beside him to give him a high five. "By the time next year comes around, you're going to be a beast."

"Going to be?" he asked, puffing out his chest. "I'm already a beast."

"Okay, big shot." Marco laughed. "You know what I mean. College ball is a different game all together. You're making gains though. You're going to kill it on the field."

"Thanks, man," Barrett said, taking his sweat towel from the bench. "On the field and in the sheets."

"Who's hitting the sheets?" Brad, one of their teammates, asked, coming over to the machine. He looked at the weight Barrett had on the bench and shook his head. Adding ten pounds to each side, he nodded to the machine. "Probably not you, seeing as how Logan dumped you," he added, casting a sideways look at Barrett.

"What did you say?" he asked, stepping forward.

"Enough, guys," Marco said, stepping between them. He cast Barrett a stern look. "Another fight, and you risk suspension. Worse than that, you're eighteen. He's not. You could be charged."

"I don't care about that," Barrett said, pushing past Marco.

"You'll lose that scholarship you busted your ass to get. Cool it!"

He hit his fist against the bench. Marco was right, but it didn't change the fact that he needed to set the record straight. Anger flowed through his veins, and all he could see was red.

Brad was laughing, carrying on about how Logan was probably seeing half the men's basketball team by now, but it was worse than that. Throwing his towel in Brad's direction, Barrett grabbed his bag and headed for the showers. He didn't have to sit around and listen to the rest of these assholes joke about it. She wasn't seeing any of the guys at school. She was probably cozied up with her new best friend, Carter, who was no doubt going to try to turn her into the picture-perfect little basketball-playing lesbian.

It would serve her right, if that's what everyone thought. In the locker room, he undressed and hopped in the shower. His anger stewed as he thought about his options. He was heartbroken, sure. He'd loved Logan, but it was bigger than that.

He'd thought a million times about texting her and apologizing, asking her to take him back. He'd even driven over to her neighborhood with good intentions one night, but he'd chickened out. What good would it even do to make contact? She'd made it clear she didn't want to be with him. All he'd be doing was giving her another chance to hurt him.

He didn't have the luxury of just saying he was sad and didn't want to talk about it. No, that would make him look weak, and he had to be the toughest of them all. A senior. A leader. The star player. There was too much riding on his shoulders to risk it. He had to save face, one way or another. Would it make him seem like less of a man if she left him for some girl? Or would it make her the center of attention and take the heat off of him? He slapped the wall in frustration. There was no way to win this. He gritted his teeth. She'd humiliated him on a night when all he'd wanted to do was let loose with some friends, have some drinks, and maybe enjoy some time with his girlfriend after the dance.

Now, some underclassman was mocking him openly, without fear of retribution, because he needed his damn scholarship. As he dried off, his mind was made up. He pulled out his phone and installed a dating app. He was going to find a rebound quickly, and he was going to mend his broken heart with a little bit of retaliation.

He opened up his Snapchat app, selected a photo from his camera roll, and typed in a few sentences. His fingers hovered over the trash icon, but he posted it anyway. Smiling to himself, he stood and got dressed. Whatever the aftermath was, it would be better than this. It had to be. He'd cried for the first time in years the other day, and he damn sure wasn't going to wait around for it to happen again.

He swiped through options of local women, selected a handful, and shot them messages. By the end of the week, he'd be posting pictures with someone else, and he'd make sure he wasn't the butt of the joke anymore.

Grabbing his bags, he stormed to his truck and peeled out of the parking lot. Logan Watts would regret the day she broke his heart and ruined their relationship and his future.

* * *

Surrounded by bags from the mall, a scattered array of wrapping paper and bows, Logan sorted through her purchases. She'd finally checked everyone off her list. Smiling to herself, she looked into the bag that held the gifts she'd selected for Carter. Ever since their date, they'd agreed to keep things moving slowly, but Logan couldn't get Carter out of her mind.

Those kisses, the feeling of their hands together, the way she smelled of earthy scents Logan couldn't quite place. All of it was perfection. She pushed the bag to the center of the room. She'd save that one for last. She wanted to take extra care to ensure it was wrapped perfectly.

A knock at the door pulled her out of her daydream.

"Hey," Ben called from the other side. "Can I come in?"

Logan heard the falter in his voice and knew something was wrong. She shoved his present under her bed. "Yeah, what's up?"

The door opened slowly, and she leaned over to see him. His face pale, and his eyes full of worry, he stood in the open doorway for a second, before stepping inside and pulling the door closed. "I know you try your best not to be on your phone all the time, so you're not a typical obsessed teen, but..." He looked down at the phone in his hand. "Have you...have you seen anything weird today?"

"What is it?" She reached for his phone, but he clutched it to his chest.

"It's"—he looked to the floor and then back to her—"about you."

"I haven't seen anything." She stood and walked over to where Ben stood. "Whatever it is, it's fine. There have been plenty of rumors that have gone around about me."

"This one is different." Ben took a seat on the edge of her bed.

"Just tell me, Ben."

"Here," he said, looking down to the floor again, handing her the phone.

She looked at the screen, then back to Ben and finally back to the phone. Her mouth fell open, and her hands started to shake. She managed only one word. "Barrett?"

Ben nodded. She gulped and stared back at the screen. He'd posted a photo he'd taken of her on the night of the dance, with text that read, "Three years, and I never knew. Congrats on coming out, Logan. Hope you and your new girlfriend are happy. As for me, I'm back on the market!"

"Ben," she said, turning her attention back to him and handing over his phone. "Barrett is just dealing with this breakup in his own way."

"How can you say that?" Ben stood up and crossed his arms over his chest. "He's deliberately trying to hurt you. He's an asshole. I'll teach him a lesson if you want me to."

Her mind was spinning, but she put her feelings aside for a second and grabbed Ben's shoulder. "I don't want that. I'm not putting you in harm's way."

"You know I'm not a fighter, but this can't stand."

"He's not worth it, Ben. It's okay."

"No, it's really not, but what are you going to do?"

The question hung in-between them as she searched for some sort of an answer. She didn't have a good one, and she didn't know that there was a good response. "I don't know," she finally admitted, "but I'll take care of it."

"Okay, what do you need from me? How can I help?"

She took a seat on the bed. "Honestly, you're already doing more than enough." She motioned for him to sit next to her. "I don't know if I tell you enough how thankful I am for you."

"You're my sister, Logan. We may have fought a lot when we were younger, but none of that matters now."

The meaning behind it wasn't lost on her. Once you lost a sibling, a lot of that other stuff became trivial. She watched all of her friends bicker with their siblings about things that she and Ben wouldn't dare to let come between them now. They were bonded by trauma.

She reached over and gave him a hug. If there were ever an opportune time to tell him, this would have been it. But, she froze. The words wouldn't come, and she didn't want to mess this up.

She stretched her neck to the side and leveled her gaze. "Truth be told, people are going to believe what they want," she said with a sigh. She was trying to convince herself as much as she was him. "I'm going to be playing college basketball, so I'm sure this won't be the first of those rumors. You know how stereotypes go." *Even if they're true*, she thought. "I'll roll with the punches. The right people will actually come to me to figure out what's going on, and no one should really care anyway."

Would they care? She clenched her jaw, her mind running rampant. No one at school really batted an eye when someone new came out, but she wasn't ready for *this*—not when she was still figuring it out. She swallowed hard. They'd all think it was a big shock, but she didn't think she'd lose friends over it, if they found out she did indeed like Carter. She closed her eyes, trying to stop the incessant thoughts.

"Why would he say that?" She looked up and met Ben's gaze. His pained expression broke her heart. He really was too pure for this world.

"People say a lot of things," she said, waving her hand through the air. Her heart raced, but she tried to keep her tone neutral. Was everyone going to believe it, and did it even matter if they did? Or, was she strong enough to let what she said to Ben stand? Ben was still staring at her, searching for answers. "I made friends with a girl in some of my classes. Carter, the one who drove me to the game, she likes girls." She paused and pulled her feet underneath her. "She also drove me home from the dance after I broke up with Barrett, and he's been jealous about it ever since."

"He's acting like a child then. You're allowed to have friends, and who cares if those friends are gay?" Ben scoffed.

He tilted his head to the side, appearing as if he'd had an epiphany, and turned to her. "If those stereotypes are true, that's okay too. You know that, right?"

"Thanks, Ben," Logan said with a nervous laugh. "Is that your way of asking?"

"Only if you want to tell. I don't believe the rumors. I'll believe what you tell me." He looked at Logan and shook his head. "Sorry, am I not supposed to ask? I don't...I..."

"I don't know the rules either, and I'm trusting you with this." She leaned in closer, making her point clear.

"I won't breathe a word of it."

She smiled, knowing it was true. Putting her hand on his shoulder, she nodded. "Barrett is an asshole," she said with a nod. "A complete and total asshole in many ways, but he's also hurting. And"—she paused, taking a deep breath—"he's not totally off base here. I didn't break up with him because of Carter. I broke up with him because I don't like him. It wasn't about her. It was about me and what I wanted. He put two and two together, and decided she must be to blame."

"Do you...like her?"

"I do." Logan nodded. Her breath came out ragged, having spoken the truth for the first time to anyone aside from Carter. "I really do."

Ben smiled. "Good, then I don't care what he says, as long as you're not upset."

"Well, I wasn't really ready to have that info out there, so just for now, keep it between you and me. But I can't really go around denying it, only to have to come clean later. I guess I'm figuring it all out as I go too."

"Okay. Offer still stands if you need me to help out."

"Thank you, Ben," she said, giving him another hug. "Are we cool?"

"Yeah," he said, standing. "I meant what I said. You're my sister, and none of the rest of the stuff matters."

"And I meant when I said you're the best. Now go on, and let me wrap your present."

He smiled, looking around the room.

"It's hidden."

"Fine," he said, looking more at ease as he headed for the door.

When the door closed behind him, she turned up her music, so he wouldn't hear the freak-out that was inevitable. She let out a heavy sigh. She'd known Barrett was angry, but in no way had she been prepared for this. If he'd posted this, everyone in school had likely seen it. That meant it was only a matter of time until the adults started talking too.

She buried her head in her hands. So much for wanting some time to figure it out. She reached for her phone, and thought about texting Carter. The onslaught of notifications was too much. Calls, texts, messages. She put her phone back on the bedside table, and forced herself to breathe.

Moving to the floor, she pulled out the gifts she'd bought for Carter. Her hands shook, but she tried to still her breathing and focus on the happiness in front of her. She opened the bag, carefully pulling out the contents—a framed Beatles album cover, a book of poetry, and a plaid scarf. She held the scarf close to her body. This was what she'd chosen, or rather, what had chosen her. She hadn't asked to have feelings for another girl. It had just happened, the same cosmic way the sun rose every morning and set every night. It was already in motion, long before the car ride.

She leaned against her bed and savored the last few minutes where she could at least pretend her world was normal. She didn't have to answer to Barrett's accusations. She could simply say they had a bad breakup, and leave it at that. No other answers would be given, because she wasn't ready to lie. But, she wasn't so sure she was ready to face the truth and the fallout that might come with it.

Pulling her phone out, she cleared away all of her notifications. She opened her texts from Josie.

What is going on?

Are you okay?

I love you no matter what, but please talk to me.

Call me!

Pick up your phone, dammit!

She closed her eyes, willing it all to go away. The words of encouragement were sweet, but it was all too much. She thought about turning off her phone, but instead typed out a reply.

I'm fine. Not sure what the deal is. I guess he's upset. Still on for dinner tomorrow?

Hitting Send, she breathed a sigh of relief. If she could just continue her life as normal, maybe people would get back to minding their own business. Besides, by the time school went back to session, there would surely be something else for everyone to focus on.

Someone had to do something stupid over the break, or maybe there would be a new couple for everyone to obsess over by the time classes resumed.

She could only hope.

CHAPTER THIRTEEN

Scents of cinnamon and anise filled the kitchen, as Carter wiped the flour from her hands. From the corner of the room, her mom hummed along to "Let it Snow" playing on the radio. She smiled and scooped the latest batch of cookies off the baking sheet.

"You make quite the sous chcf," her mom said, coming up beside her to admire the perfectly shaped biscochitos—a holiday tradition in their household. "In fact, you might beat me out of a job one of these days. You'll get to take over the holiday traditions and baking."

"I like being the helper." Carter moved past her to put the cookies into the oven. "It's all about having the right company," she added, hopping up onto the one spot on the counter that wasn't covered with flour.

"Speaking of the right company, how are things going with that girl from the night of the dance?"

"Mom," Carter said, playfully throwing a dishtowel in her direction.

"What?" Her mom turned with her hand on her hip and stared at Carter. "You can't blame me for asking. You're sealed up tighter than Fort Knox. I have to work to get anything out of you." She turned back toward the counter, where she was putting the final touches on their last batch of Christmas candies. "What did you get her for Christmas?"

"I see right through the change in approach," Carter said, laughing as she leaned back against the cabinets. Out of respect for Logan's privacy, Carter had refrained from even telling Aiden about their shared kiss and their texts back and forth each day. Now she took a deep breath. This was her safe space, and she knew how lucky she was to have that in a mother. "I did get her a gift."

"I knew it! What did you get her?"

"The thing is, she's more than a friend." Carter dodged the question. "But I don't think she's ready for anyone else to know that."

"Honey, anyone with eyes can deduce what they want. I saw the way she looked at you that night. The girl's got it bad."

"She's not the only one," Carter admitted. "I really like her, but I don't want to mess it up."

"Okay, then, what did you get her for Christmas?"

"It sounds so silly when I say it out loud." Carter covered her face with her hands.

"If it sounds silly, it probably means it's heartfelt. You don't have to share if you don't want to. Just make her feel special."

"Thanks," Carter said. She hopped down from the counter. "Can I take her some of the biscochitos to go with her gift?"

"Only if you wrap them nicely and present them in a fashion worthy of coming from this household." Her mom smiled, as she handed over the Christmas tree-printed beeswax wraps and a bundle of ribbon. "Remember, it's all about making sure it's heartfelt."

Carter set to work pulling in a dozen of the cookies from her first batch and wrapping them with a bow. "I'll be home later," she called out, as she collected the rest of the packages from the hallway and headed for the door.

On my way. She sent the text before pulling the car out of the drive and heading for Logan's.

She'd seen the photo that had been circulating, and she'd talked to Logan since. Logan had assured her everything had mostly blown over, and that people were now talking about the new girl from a couple of towns over Barrett had been posting pictures with, but she wasn't sure. It was a lot to come out, and to have someone do it for you was just unfair. On top of that, this was their first time hanging out since their date, and she was nervous all over again.

She looked over at the package of cookies in the passenger seat, next to the other gifts she'd carefully selected. Would cookies, presents, and maybe a kiss be enough to assuage Logan's very real fears? Or, would it be a Christmas celebration marred by Barrett's selfishness and ego? She put the car in park, and waited outside. She'd give anything to waltz up to the door, presents in hand, but she knew that wasn't their deal. They'd agreed to go out under the guise of last minute shopping, so Logan didn't have to explain anything to her dad.

She picked up her phone to text, but Logan bounded out the front door before she could type.

"Merry Christmas," she said, opening the door, holding a package wrapped in red and white striped paper, with a large red bow on top.

In an instant, Carter's worries faded. She'd make sure to be by Logan's side through every step of the journey, but the smile on Logan's face told her it was okay.

"Merry Christmas to you," she said, moving the cookies and presents to the back seat. "Where should we go?"

"I was thinking maybe downtown," Logan said, climbing in and fastening her seatbelt. "That way we could exchange presents and then grab a couple of things to take for a dinner in the foothills. I know you have to be back before too late to celebrate with your mom, and I should be back too."

"You don't have a big Christmas Eve dinner you're skipping out on, do you?"

"We do our big celebration on Christmas morning," Logan said, reaching for Carter's hand. "I want to spend today with you, as long as that's cool with you."

"More than cool." Carter put the car in gear and headed toward downtown.

"How are you holding up?" she asked, as Logan played with the music.

"I'm mostly fine," she said, looking out the window briefly. "People really didn't press too much. I'm sure there are still rumors going around, but no one is really bugging me anymore. That's nice. It takes the pressure off me, and just puts it out there." She gripped Carter's hand tighter. "It's okay if they believe what they want to believe. They're not wrong. I do like you, and for now, I don't have to explain that to anyone."

"That's a really healthy way to look at it, as my mom would say." Carter smiled. The woman really was wise, and that level of emotional maturity had helped Carter through a lot of really difficult times.

"Does your mom know where you are?"

"Today she does." Carter nodded. She pulled into a parking lot and put the car in park. "She's sworn to secrecy."

"Thank you for that," Logan said, pulling the gift box from the back seat. "Just a little something for you."

Carter smiled, accepting the box. "Do I go first?"

Logan nodded. "I'm really the worst with keeping gifts a secret, so I want you to open it now." She bit her lip and watched as Carter gently removed the bow and ripped into the wrapping paper. She pulled out the album cover first, holding it close to her heart.

"How did you know this was my favorite album?"

"I gathered from your playlists," Logan said, her smile lighting up as she looked from the gift to Carter. "You really like it?"

"I love it. It'll go nicely on my bedroom wall." It was a room Logan had yet to see, but the album cover paired perfectly with her décor. She pulled out the book and smiled. "Thank you. Maybe we can read this together sometime?"

"I'd like that."

As she pulled out the scarf, she ran her fingers along the soft material. "This is perfect."

"You were wearing plaid," Logan said, reaching out to touch the material.

"What?"

"The day you first caught my eye—like, in *that* way, you were wearing plaid. So, whenever I saw this in the store, it made me blush a bit, and I just had to see it on you."

Carter smiled, loosening the scarf she had on, and draping the new one around her neck. "And what do you think?"

"I think you definitely catch my eye." Logan wrapped her hands around both sides of the scarf and pulled Carter in for a kiss.

"I love it all," she said, pulling away after a second. "Thank you. Now"—she reached into the back seat of the car—"your turn." Carter handed her the cookies first. "These were made with care this morning, for you to enjoy later," she said, before handing her the larger package.

Logan looked at her, smiling as she tore into the paper. When the gift came into view, her mouth dropped open. "I love this," she said, gently running her fingers over the frame.

Carter looked at it once more, even though she'd stared at it a hundred times trying to decide if it was a fitting gift. She'd taken the photo of their Converse at the dance and edited it to make the colors pop, before printing an eight by ten and framing it.

"I'm hanging this on my wall too," she said, smiling once more at the picture and then at Carter. "Thank you."

"There's this one too," Carter said, handing her another package.

"There's more?" Logan crinkled her nose and shook her head. "This was more than enough."

"Open it," Carter said, nodding toward the package.

Following instructions, Logan opened the box and pulled out the sweatshirt Carter had rush ordered with Logan's last name on the back and the UNM logo on the front.

Logan held it to her chest and leaned over for another quick kiss. "Thank you." She pulled off her leather jacket, tossing it in the back seat, before slipping the hooded sweatshirt over her head. "A perfect fit." She smiled at Carter, showcasing the front of the sweatshirt like she was in a game show. "Do you like it?"

"It looks great," Carter said, watching every one of Logan's movements with awe. It didn't matter if she was in a ball gown or a sweatshirt. She was stunning. "So, where to?"

"I'm thinking we hit the market, grab some picnic stuff, and then go sit out by the mountains, so we can have a little alone time."

Carter's body tingled at the thought of more alone time. Keeping her hands to herself during their movie date had been all but torture, glorious torture. She took a deep breath and nodded. Even if she'd wanted to, she was pretty sure she couldn't have denied Logan's request. "Let's do it," she agreed.

As they shopped through the small, local market, Carter tried to focus on picking out the right items for their picnic, but choosing meats and cheeses seemed so frivolous when Logan was right behind her, close enough to touch.

"I love these," Logan said, picking up a box of crackers. "These will pair well with our spread. Don't you think?"

Carter nodded and held out the cart for Logan to drop the crackers inside. "Whatever you want." Even as she spoke the words, she realized Logan probably didn't know the depths. Whatever Logan wanted, she'd do everything in her power to make it a reality. The smile she got whenever Logan was happy was more than enough motivation. As Logan debated over which type of fruit 'felt like Christmas,' Carter pulled out her phone. After a quick check of her bank account, in which she'd saved birthday and Christmas money for years, she smiled.

"Do you have maybe an hour after our picnic before you have to get back?"

Logan's eyes sparkled with curiosity. She nodded. "I could make time. What do you have in mind?"

"A surprise," she said, raising an eyebrow as she hid the screen of her phone and purchased tickets. When the confirmation email came in, she took a screenshot and slid her phone back into her pocket, her heart soaring with possibility. Maybe she was a hopeless romantic, but she'd always dreamed of taking a date on the Sandia Peak Tramway. What could be sweeter than soaring over the desert to the top of the Sandia Mountains, amid a star-filled sky, and on Christmas Eve, no less? It would be a dream come true. She glanced at Logan, who held up pomegranate seeds and grapes, lifting each one separately, as though trying to weigh the benefits of one over the other.

"Get the grapes," Carter said, imagining what it would look like to watch Logan pop them into her mouth. She blushed, hoping Logan couldn't read through her words to the sensual image she'd concocted.

"Grapes, it is!" Logan exclaimed. "Let me get this," she said, sliding in front to grab the cart.

Carter thought about resisting, but Logan had a hand on her hip. "You treated me to dinner after the dance, and you cooked for me. The least I can do is pick up our picnic supplies."

"Okay fine," Carter said, relinquishing the cart. "But after dinner is my treat."

"You're the treat," Logan said, winking as she headed to pay for the items. Carter's heart skipped a beat. One day, she'd find a way to tell Logan what that move did to her, but for today, she'd keep it as her little, tantalizing secret. She watched as Logan loaded the items onto the conveyor belt and paid the cashier. As they made their way back to the car, Logan looped her arm through Carter's.

"Aren't you worried someone might see?" Carter asked, checking their surroundings.

"I'm not worried about anything right now," Logan said, pulling her closer, so their hips touched. "I'm just enjoying a joyous Christmas Eve."

"It's already the best one I've ever had." Carter looped her fingers through Logan's and smiled.

"Me too," Logan agreed, turning her head to look into Carter's eyes, "and that's saying a lot, considering one year, on Christmas Eve, I got a go-cart as an early Christmas present."

"You're saying I'm better than a go-cart?"

"I'd say so," Logan said, a slow smile creeping onto her lips. "I mean, you get me places a lot faster than that go-cart did." She stopped and laughed out loud. "That sounded dirtier when I said it out loud than I meant for it to." She blushed, breaking contact to get into the passenger side. "But it's true. You also make me feel even more alive than I felt at ten, racing through the wide-open spaces in the field behind our house."

Carter laughed. "I know what you mean." The innuendo included, she thought, climbing into the front seat. As she put the car in gear and headed north, instead of east toward the foothill trails, Logan scrunched up her nose.

"Where are we going?"

"I'm taking us to a different trailhead for the picnic, so we'll be closer to the after-dinner events." She watched Logan out of the corner of her eyes, noting the way her eyes lit up with curiosity.

"You keep me on my toes," she said after a minute, pulling a grape from the paper bag and munching on it. "Do you want one?" She held out a single grape. "Consider it an appetizer."

As if her earlier fantasy was coming to life in real time, Logan reached over and placed the grape against Carter's lips. Opening her mouth, she accepted the gift with a smile.

Gripping the steering wheel, she chewed the grape and focused on the road, even though everything in her body wanted to pull the car over and take Logan in her arms.

"You're something else," she said, as she swallowed. "How do you do *that* to me, just by feeding me a snack?"

"Oh, you liked that?" Logan asked playfully, pulling another grape from the bag with a devious smile. "Does it give you that racing through a field in a go-cart feeling?"

"Yeah." Carter nodded. "It's a mix of adrenaline and intimacy, peppered with this feeling of complete ecstasy."

"That's how it felt when I kissed you," Logan said. She looked out the window, before bringing another grape to Carter's lips. "It drove me crazy, waiting to kiss you, when that's all I wanted. But once I did, it drove me crazy to stop. The need to feel your lips on mine is kind of insatiable."

"I know the feeling."

Logan cleared her throat and stared down at the grapes. "There will be more of those in a minute," she said, placing the bag on the floorboard. "For now, can I just say that it's both weird and amazing to be able to put these things into words with you and not worry about what you'll think?" She paused and shook her head. "That maybe came out wrong. I care about what you think, but I don't think you'll judge me when I admit how I feel."

"I could never judge that." Carter reached over to put a reassuring hand on Logan's knee.

Logan placed her hand over Carter's and smiled. "I appreciate that."

"Me too," Carter said, gently caressing her leg. "The start of any strong relationship is communication." She laughed. "That's what my mom says anyway, and judging by her failed relationship with my dad, who left when I was I was thirteen, she always says the communication wasn't open and honest."

"She's a smart lady," Logan said with a nod. "I really enjoyed meeting her."

"Maybe one night, you can join us for dinner." As soon as the words were out of her mouth, she stiffened. They hadn't even finished their second date, and she was bringing up hanging out with her family. "If you want to, that is. Not right now, but maybe sometime in the future."

Logan smiled. "Awkward looks cute on you too," she said, grabbing the bag of grapes and selecting a large, round one. She ran her fingers over the skin and popped it in her mouth, keeping her eyes on Carter the entire time. "I'd like to hang out with your mom sometime," she added after a moment. "We'll figure all that out, but I'm not planning on going anywhere."

The words soothed the fears that Carter hadn't been able to let go of, that at some point, Logan would wise up and realize Carter had just been nothing more than an experiment. She slid her hand up to rest in Logan's.

As they pulled into the parking lot of the trail, Carter grabbed the blanket she had brought along and stepped from the car. The chill in the wind intensified, and she wrapped her coat tighter around her. Turning back, she grabbed Logan's jacket from the back seat. "You might need this, as well," she said, draping it over Logan's shoulders.

"Thank you." Logan turned to her. The grocery bag created a barrier, but she leaned forward and brought her lips against Carter's for a long, slow kiss. "I think I'll find ways to keep warm," she added, pulling away and heading to the entrance of the trail.

In a clearing, just off the parking lot, Carter spread the thick flannel blanket onto the ground and took a look around. Beside her, Logan laid out the spread, as if she was preparing for a food magazine shoot. Carefully arranging, then rearranging the items, she bit her lip and leaned back, before nodding her head.

"Dinner is served," she said, holding out her hands to unveil her handiwork.

Logan leaning back on her heels, dressed in a present from Carter, and surrounded by the snow-covered trees, amidst the backdrop of the mountains, was a sight to see. "Looks incredible," she commented, looking directly at Logan instead of the food.

Logan looked up to meet her gaze and blushed. "Have a seat," she said, nodding to the spot next to her. "Maybe we should save these," she noted, grabbing the grapes and placing them into her lap, "for dessert. You know, give you something to look forward to at the end of the meal."

Her body tensed at how Logan looked at her, with such direct and unyielding adoration. Nodding, she grabbed a cracker from the center of the blanket and popped it into her mouth.

"I know a picnic in the snow is a bit impractical," Logan said, glancing around at the stillness of the winter evening. "I think, judging from our lack of company, we're the only two crazy enough to deem it a good idea. But, thanks for going along with it." Logan grabbed a cube of cheese. "It's been one of the things I've always wanted to do on a date."

"Funny you should mention that," Carter said, checking the time on her phone. "In about forty-five minutes, I get to show you one of my bucket list date ideas."

Logan smiled, taking a bite and shaking her head. "You're too good to me."

"That's nonsense." Carter leaned back to look into Logan's eyes, hoping she'd hear the sincerity in her voice. "You deserve every good thing, no matter what anyone has told you in the past."

Logan sighed, leaning over to rest her head on Carter's chest, and in that moment, Carter was certain she'd never experienced anything as close to magic as she was right now.

CHAPTER FOURTEEN

As they finished their picnic, Logan reached behind her, pulling the package of cookies Carter had so carefully wrapped to the front of the blanket. She smiled and unwrapped the ribbon.

"Dessert," she said, "thanks to you."

She took a cookie, examining the perfect Zia symbol in its center. "These look amazing."

"They taste even better," Carter said, proudly biting into a cookie. "Thanks to my mom. It's her abuelita's recipe. I just helped make them."

Logan took a bite, savoring the mix of spices on her tongue. She nodded. "You're right. They're delicious."

Carter finished her cookie, and Logan let out a laugh. "You have a few crumbs," she said, pointing to her own lip to show Carter where they were.

Running her tongue along her bottom lip, Carter raised an eyebrow.

Logan's heart pounded, and she leaned forward. "Maybe I should help," she said, her voice husky. Everything about this night was perfection, and she didn't think she could resist any longer. Pressing her lips against Carter's, she tangled her hands in Carter's hair and pulled Carter on top of her. Need built inside of her, as their bodies collided. The kiss deepened, and she gently bit Carter's bottom lip.

Keep it vertical. She heard the words of the youth pastor from the church her parents attended a handful of times in the back of her mind and stifled a laugh. His teaching had always been that, once things went horizontal, it was difficult to curb the desire to have premarital sex. When Carter was around, it was difficult to keep her thoughts from going in that direction in a grocery store. Against her kiss, Carter let out a low moan, and she pulled back. "Are you okay?"

"I'm…" Carter took a deep breath and pressed her lips together in an o-shape. She let out a sigh. "I'm more than okay." Carter smiled and leaned back down. She trailed her lips lower, kissing Logan's neck, and for the first time, Logan understood why people liked the move. Before it had felt sloppy and unnecessary. But now, it made total sense. Every nerve in her body felt raw, like a current of electricity was shooting through her. Leaning her head back, she looked up at the stars and sighed.

"If we don't pack up now," she said, reluctantly pulling Carter up so she could stare into her eyes, "we're going to miss your dream date. I wouldn't dare take that away from you."

"This might be my new dream date," Carter said, laughing as she moved to a sitting position. She took a long drink of her water bottle and shook her head. "How the hell do you do that?"

"And what would *that* be?" Logan asked knowingly. She wanted to hear Carter say it.

"You know exactly what you're doing to me."

"I do," Logan agreed. "But only because you're doing the same thing to me." She brought her thumbnail up to her mouth and nibbled on it, only to catch herself. She wasn't nervous, but she was definitely undone. It was as if the earth had moved beneath her, showing her a whole new world she had yet to explore. "All those things I thought were broken or missing make a lot more sense now," she said, taking a deep breath and trying to return her heart rate to normal.

"Yeah?" Beside her, Carter slowly popped a grape into her mouth, and Logan smiled. Now she got it. Who would have thought the simple act of eating fruit could be so alluring? She was pretty sure Carter could do anything and make it look like the hottest thing on the planet.

"Yeah," she said after a moment. "It's like I'd hear the other girls talk about how difficult it was to wait to have sex…" She trailed off, taking a sip of her water. "Is it okay to talk about sex?"

Carter pressed her lips together but couldn't hide her grin. "It is," she said, dragging out the words. "Have you ever?"

"Talked about it?" Logan shook her head. "Aside from being asked and saying 'no,' I haven't. There really wasn't a need to talk about it, because I didn't want to do it." She gulped. "And, no. I haven't had sex." Did Carter want to have sex with her too? She looked up at the sky. Was she ready? Was it too soon? It was probably too soon to even be thinking about it. There were so many questions, but nothing made sense when Carter kissed her. None of the answers made a difference. All she felt was the connection. "Have you?" she asked quietly.

Beside her, Carter looped her hand through Logan's. She nodded. "I have, and it's okay to talk about it. It's also okay to wait on that. I'm in no hurry."

"Do you…" Logan trailed off. This was so unlike situations she'd been in before, where she suddenly felt safe and free to express her emotions and concerns in a romantic setting. "Do you want to?" she asked, relying on her last bit of courage to speak the question.

"When the time is right," Carter said, planting a kiss on her forehead. "There's no rush. Think of it like a basketball game." Carter smiled, and Logan had to fight the urge to kiss her all over again. "It takes time to lay the foundation for the game. You don't just jump to the fourth quarter for a buzzer beater shot."

"Don't people usually use baseball and the bases in that reference?"

"Some do, but I was being accommodating for my audience." She laughed and glanced at her phone. "Besides, we need to head up the road a couple of miles."

Standing, Logan gathered the items. The rush in her body still lingered, but now her head was swimming with questions. How would she know when the time was right? If her body was in charge, right now was the perfect time. But, was it more complicated than that? She made a mental note to ask Carter later. She wasn't going to mess up their date night by adding pressure or tension where it wasn't needed. Carter was right. There was time for that in the future.

As they put the items in the back seat and climbed into the car, Carter took her hand. "I'm glad you feel safe to talk to me," she said, squeezing Logan's hand. "We can figure it all out together."

On the drive, Carter put on the Beatles and turned the volume low enough that Logan could still talk if she wanted to, but Logan watched the night sky outside her window instead. She was sure if she looked back to Carter, she'd cry at the mere thought of how sweet and understanding she was in moments of uncertainty.

When Carter pulled into the parking lot of the Tram, Logan's eyes widened. "I haven't been here since I was a kid!"

"I haven't been in years either. Last time I was on here, it was a cold, wintery night, and I was in that awkward early teen stage. I was completely in my head about every girl I saw, and I was certain that it would make the most romantic date night." Carter smiled. "That was before I saw what a snowy Christmas Eve picnic looked like though. That'll be hard to top."

"Well, let's go find out," Logan said, bounding from the car. With renewed energy, she felt like a little kid again. Grabbing Carter's hand, she raced up the steps.

As Carter presented the tickets to the cashier and they climbed onto the small car, Logan couldn't hide her excitement. Around them, a small crowd gathered into the car, and the ride's operator donned a Santa hat. "Merry Christmas, everyone," he called out, shutting the doors. Thankful they weren't the only ones around, so his attention wasn't directed at them, Logan made her way to the far side of the car and grabbed Carter's hand.

Pulling Carter close against her, she held her for a moment, before stepping behind her and putting her arms around Carter's waist. If this was Carter's dream date, she was going to do everything she could to make sure it felt as romantic and amazing as Carter had envisioned.

Around them, people chattered, taking in the sights, and Logan leaned forward, placing a single kiss on Carter's cheek.

"It's perfect," Carter whispered.

"Everything you dreamed of?"

"More." Carter's answer was simple, but full of awe. Logan was sure Carter could feel the pounding of her heart, but she didn't care. If there was ever a time to be raw and vulnerable, it was when falling for someone.

Falling. She played with the word in her head. It was such a strange word to think of, while soaring thousands of feet over the great expanses below. Truth be told, she didn't think falling was the right word to explain how she felt. Soaring might be more accurate. She wasn't falling for Carter. She was reaching new heights, flying through the air over the things she'd thought she knew to be true, and discovering new feelings, new sensations, new fears.

Whatever it was, she never wanted to let go. The thought alone caused her to momentarily lose her grip on Carter, as fear gripped her heart. Was it too much too soon? Straightening her shoulders for a second, she leaned back in and resumed her snuggled-up position, wrapping Carter even tighter. She was moving fast, and she knew she'd have to sort out these emotions at some point, but just as their car moved slowly up to the mountaintop with no way to return it before it got to the top, she was certain there was no way to slow down the trajectory of her feelings. Nor did she want to.

Behind her, she heard a couple of whispers. Glancing over her shoulder, she saw an elderly woman watching them. Her heart fell, as she glanced back to Carter. Expecting dismay, she turned back to the older woman, who offered a sweet smile.

"There's nothing like young love," the woman said quietly. "Savor it."

Logan smiled, nodding. She turned her attention back to Carter who had her face close to the glass, watching every detail. She wanted to tell her about the woman, but figured the word *love* wasn't something she should utter just yet. She'd said it before when she didn't mean it, and that wasn't a mistake she was going to be making again.

As the tramway car reached the top of the mountain, they were instructed to be back on in thirty minutes for a return trip to the station. Carter took Logan's hand, smiling from ear to ear, as they exited.

"Want to grab a quick drink at the little restaurant up here?" Carter asked, her eyes shimmering with hope.

"They won't serve you without an ID," Logan teased. "But yeah, let's go grab something."

"I wasn't talking about alcohol," Carter said, pulling her off to the side, where they were alone for a second. "Look around," she said, waving her hands out in front of her, showcasing the scenic views of the city lights sprawled around them, thousands of feet below. "Being here with you, with these views, is intoxicating enough."

Pulling her behind the backdrop of a sign, Logan nodded. "That it is," she said, bringing her lips inches from Carter's and smiling. "What do you say we make this memory even more romantic?"

Carter raised an eyebrow and nodded. Not needing any further encouragement, Logan kissed Carter slowly and softly, savoring the taste of her lips. It might not have been the type of savoring the elderly lady had suggested, but it was good enough for Logan.

"Let's get that drink," she said after a moment. Rounding the corner, she opened the door and ushered Carter inside. The bar was covered in windows overlooking the land below, and every table adorned in Christmas décor.

"It's perfect," Carter said, her voice barely above a whisper. "Even better than I imagined."

"What would you like?" Logan asked, looking up and down the menu. "Think they'd make us a couple of virgin drinks?" She bit her lip, just saying the word *virgin*. It shouldn't be a buzzword. Virginity was nothing more than a construct, she knew, but on a night where sex had taken the focus of her mind, she blushed.

"Let's see," Carter said, not missing a beat.

As the waiter walked up to the table, Carter turned and offered a smile. "Do you have any good mocktails?"

Mocktails. A much better choice in wording. Logan nodded, as the waiter listed off a couple of options. Carter selected a mojito spin-off. Logan watched as she played with the edge of the menu, before handing it over to the waiter.

"I'll do the same," Logan said, realizing she hadn't been listening to a word he'd said.

When their drinks came, Logan glanced to Carter and to her phone. "Do you mind if we take a picture?" Logan asked.

"I'd love to," Carter agreed easily, grabbing her drink and looking around for the best angle. "Here," she said, angling their bodies to capture the view of the tram behind them. "Cheers," she said, raising her glass into the picture, before clicking the button.

"Will you send that to me?" Logan asked, playing with the straw in her glass before taking a sip.

"I will." Carter popped the photo into a text message and sent it over. "And, I'll do you one better and print it for you," Carter said, reaching below the table to grab Logan's hand.

"More décor for my room." Logan smiled. She glanced down at her phone, opening the text. "And something sweet to look at when you're not around," she added, admiring the photo.

They sipped their drinks and paid, and on the return trip, they switched positions, so Logan could be closer to the window. By the time they returned to the car, Logan couldn't remember a time she'd felt more aware of every ounce of happiness flowing through her body.

"I really thought date number one was going to be hard to beat," Logan said, laughing as they climbed into the car. "But, date number two was pretty spectacular."

"Maybe we can keep the streak alive for date number three," Carter suggested. "Do you have plans for New Year's Eve?"

Logan closed her eyes, picturing it. They'd dress up and kiss to bring in a new year, full of new possibilities. Her thoughts came to a crashing halt, when she remembered she couldn't. She frowned.

"It's okay if you have plans," Carter said, tilting her head to the side. "What's up?"

"I do have plans." Logan shook her head. "I made them months ago, or I'd totally bail out on it."

"That's fine. You're allowed to do things with your friends."

"I'd rather be with you," Logan admitted. "What are you going to do?"

"I'm not sure." Carter ran her fingers through her hair. "I haven't made any concrete plans. I may go with Alexis and Aiden to do something, or I might stay in with my mom, order a bunch of food and watch the ball drop."

"What did you have in mind if we celebrated together?" She knew it was a tease, but she wanted to see Carter's vision, to dream with her about the possibilities.

"I assume it would have involved some version of celebrating, maybe some funny hats and dressy clothing, and definitely some of these," Carter said, scooting closer and coming in for a kiss.

"Maybe I could cancel," Logan said.

"No." Carter shook her head. "I don't want that. I don't want to consume all of your time and take away time that you already have planned out. What are your plans?"

Logan sighed, wishing her friends didn't make such a big deal of planning everything months in advance. "Josie is throwing a party. Do you want to come?"

"Don't you think that might blow your cover a bit too soon?"

Logan bit her bottom lip and thought through the possibilities. It did blur a line, but it also was an opportunity to prove that they liked to hang out, to normalize Carter being part of the group. "I don't know," she said after a moment. "Consider it. If you want to come, I'd love to have you there."

"Okay," Carter said, nodding slowly. "Who all is going to be there?"

"Most of the basketball team, a lot of the football guys, a handful of other kids from school. Josie doesn't do anything small."

"I'll think about it," Carter agreed. "But nothing set in stone. I need to think on it."

"Fair enough." Logan reached for Carter's hand. "If you decide to do your own thing, we'll make date number three incredible whenever we get to have it."

"Deal."

As Carter drove, Logan turned up the music, basking in the beauty of all that the night had held. When they pulled into her driveway, she wished the night could continue, but knew it was time to let Carter get back home.

"Merry Christmas, Carter Shaw."

"Same to you, Logan Watts," Carter said with a smile. "And thank you for the best Christmas I've had in a long time."

"Thank you too." She leaned in for a goodnight kiss, but pulled back. The curtains were open in the living room, and she didn't want to have to answer questions. "Later?" she asked, hoping she hadn't hurt Carter's feelings.

"There's no rush," Carter said gently. "Go celebrate, and I'll text you later."

Logan gathered her things and got out of the car. She reached back in, to hold Carter's hand for one second longer, before heading for the door. Carter waited until she was safely inside, before pulling out of the driveway and heading for home.

With her hands full of packages, Logan slid them into the darkened hallway, not wanting to draw attention, and headed for the kitchen. In the entryway, she stopped. Her jaw fell open.

"Mom!" She ran to cover the distance between them and wrapped her arms around her mom, who was standing in front of the cabinets, sipping on a mug of hot cocoa.

"Oh, sweetheart," her mom said, leaning into the embrace and wiping a tear from her eye. "I've missed you so much."

"I missed you too! When did you get in?"

"I just got back about an hour ago. Your dad said you were out doing some last minute shopping. Did you find anything good?"

Logan remembered her cover story and nodded. "I did. I'm sorry I missed your arrival."

"Don't sweat it." She waved a hand through the air. "It was a surprise for everyone."

"Are you back for good?" Her heart fell. "Oh no, is Grandma okay?"

"Your grandma is fine. She wouldn't let me stay through Christmas. She said she'd be okay, and the hospital assured me that she'd have a lot of company on Christmas Day. I'm only here through the twenty-sixth, but I wanted to be here with you all."

"This really is the best Christmas," Logan said, wrapping her in another hug. Start to finish, it might have been the best day of her life.

Her mom kissed the top of her head and took a step back, looking her up and down.

"This is new," she said, grabbing Logan's sweatshirt. "I like it. Where did you get it?"

"It was a Christmas gift from one of my friends." The sentence sounded weird, even to her. Her mom knew all of her friends by name, but she didn't press.

"Very nice," she said, nodding. She leaned back and eyed Logan curiously. "You look so happy. Fill me in on all that I missed."

Logan looked around the room, where her dad was smiling and making a huge dinner and Ben grinned at her, slyly pointing to her sweater and giving a thumbs-up.

"I will," she said, reaching over and snagging a Christmas cookie from the counter. "In time. For now, I'm just so happy you're home."

As laughter, Christmas music, and the smell of food permeated the air, Logan was sure this was the happiest Christmas in the history of the holiday, for a number of reasons.

CHAPTER FIFTEEN

A sandalwood candle flickered in the corner of her room, and Carter sang along with Fletcher playing over her speakers, as she put the finishing touches on her outfit for the night.

Her phone buzzed with an incoming text message. She smiled, seeing Logan's name pop up on the screen.

I hope you have so much fun tonight. She read the text and grinned at the screen.

It would be more fun if she was hanging out with Logan, but she avoided saying that. There was no need to add any guilt or pressure on the night. She'd meant it when she told Logan not to cancel. And, thanks to Aiden's urging and her mom having a date for the evening, she was going to hang out with her friends after all.

Admiring her outfit once more in the mirror, she smiled and nodded. She was overdressed for a night that would no doubt end up in Aiden's basement, playing Mario Kart, but she didn't care. She adjusted the black vest over her white button-down shirt and turned to check her tailored slacks in the mirror.

Paired with her sparkling gold nail polish, it was just the right amount of over-the-top.

While she wouldn't give in to guilt, she wasn't above a bit of flirting. Snapping a quick picture in the mirror, she added it to the text message.

I hope you do too! Can't wait to see you again.

DAMN! Logan's reply came quickly, causing Carter to blush.

While you're printing out photos, I want a copy of that one! Logan replied again, before Carter could respond.

I think I can make that happen, she typed out. *Have a good time tonight, and I'll call you around midnight.*

It wouldn't be as sweet as a midnight kiss, but it would be good to hear Logan's voice.

She heard a knock at her bedroom door.

"Come in," she called, turning down the music.

Her mom stepped into the room, dressed in a formfitting black dress with a moderate slit up the side.

"You look good," Carter said, nodding in approval and rotating her hand, signaling for her mom to do a turn. "I hope you have fun tonight."

"You sure it's not too much?" Her mom did a half twirl and turned back to her, a nervous smile on her face.

"Not at all." Carter walked over and gave her a quick hug. "You look perfect. Just go and have fun."

Her mom shook her head. "I'm supposed to be the one giving you those pep talks." She stepped back and looked Carter up and down. "*You* look amazing," she added. "What's on the agenda for the evening?"

Her mom was stalling, and she knew it. She'd said she needed to leave by six, and it was already six fifteen. She indulged it for a moment though, hoping to calm her mom's nerves. She could count on both hands the number of times her mom had gone on dates since her father left. "Just going to grab dinner with Aiden and Alexis. Afterward, we'll probably hang out at Aiden's place."

"Video games and the usual? What about Logan?"

Carter cleared her throat and shook her head. "She's going to some big party."

"Oh, honey, are things okay there?" Concern colored her expression, and she reached out to grab Carter's arm.

Carter laughed. "Things are fine, Mom. She already had plans, and she invited me to join. It's just not really my crowd."

"That's fine, healthy even, to have your own friends and your own activities." She looked down at the floor. "There's a lot of weird pressure on New Year's Eve dates anyway."

"Is that why you're nervous?" She eased into the conversation, knowing her mother wouldn't be able to shy away from it forever.

"Am I that obvious?"

"You're in here, asking about video games, instead of going on the date you were so excited about yesterday."

"Is this weird for you?" Her mom said, shaking her head. "I don't want to put you in a weird position."

"Dad left years ago, Mom." Carter shook her head, giving her mother another hug. "I see him maybe twice a year on a good year. I understand that relationship is over and that's not changing. I'm well-adjusted enough to know that you are a thriving woman who deserves to make new connections. I want you to go out and be happy. That's healthy. Not dating because of me—or because things didn't work out with Dad—isn't healthy."

"How did you get so smart?"

"I had a good teacher," Carter said, smiling and grabbing her mom's hand. "At the end of the day, I just want you to be happy. Now go. You've already kept him waiting, and I'm sure he's starting to wonder if you're even going to show up."

"You're right." She turned to go, but stopped halfway to the door. "I know it's starting out as just a normal night, but if you need a ride for any reason, call me."

It had been their deal since she was a kid, anytime she was away from home, especially as she got into her teen years.

"I will, Mom," she promised, shutting the door behind her.

She tidied her room and grabbed her wallet. As if on a timer, Aiden bounded through the front door.

"Wow," he said, looking at her with an approving nod. "I feel a little underdressed." He looked down at his own jeans and Henley.

"Don't. I just wanted to dress up. I'm trying out a new look."

"Well I, for one, love it. If you're looking to pick up any of the ladies out on the town tonight, you won't have any trouble."

"No, I'm good, thanks." Her heart pounded. It wasn't easy to keep something as big as her relationship with Logan a secret, but she felt like she needed to for the time being.

"Really? Why the fancy outfit then?" He raised an eyebrow and leaned in close. "Is there something you're not telling me?"

"No." She laughed, dismissing the comment. "It's not that. I just wanted to look nice. For myself."

Her phone buzzed. She pulled it out of her pocket, careful to keep it out of Aiden's line of sight without him noticing her sneaking around.

Working to keep a neutral expression, she was sure her eyes widened at the sight of Logan, clad in black leather pants and an off-the-shoulder, scoop-neck maroon shirt.

"I forgot something in my room," she said, bolting for the stairs. "I'll be right down."

"Mmmhmm," he said, narrowing his eyes at her.

She was going to have to learn to be more discreet at some point, but right now, all she needed was a minute of privacy.

With the door closed behind her, she pulled up the picture again and stared.

"I'm one lucky girl," she whispered.

You are stunning she replied. *Thanks for the visual.*

Logan's lips were painted in a deep rose color, and Carter wanted nothing more than to feel them press against her own. She took a deep breath and closed out of the message. With another look in the mirror, she headed back downstairs.

"What was that all about?" Aiden pressed, leaning up against the stair rail.

"My ChapStick," she said, reaching into her pocket and showing him the tube. "Can't go around with dry lips, when it's freezing outside."

He nodded, his raised eyebrow telling her that he didn't buy it but was going to let it slide.

"Where to?" she asked, changing the subject.

"After we pick up Alexis, I thought we'd hit downtown. Maybe we can get a taste of the wild side as we watch other people party. Then, we can go to my house. We can plan something new and exciting over dinner, or we can do the usual. Video games and snacks."

"Works for me." She locked up the house and followed him to the car.

"And on the drive, you can fill me in on where you've been all break."

"You've been in Connecticut with your dad's family," she corrected. "I've been here the whole time."

"Yeah and mysteriously busy."

"I've been hanging out with my mom a lot." It was the truth. Aside from the couple of times she'd hung out with Logan, she'd pretty much spent her entire break at the house.

"Why all the sudden interest in being a homebody?"

"I've always been a homebody." She shrugged, buckling her seatbelt. "Besides, she's been going through some changes, and I wanted to be here for her."

"Oh, like menopause?"

"Not like menopause," she said, laughing and shaking her head. "She's on a date tonight, and with me possibly leaving next year, it's just a lot. I've just wanted to be home more often." That, and she was the only one with whom Carter could really open up and talk about her feelings about everything she was experiencing for the first time.

Her only other forays into a romantic life had been an after-class hookup with a girl in her summer arts program and a couple of kisses here and there while she was figuring out what she wanted. This was a totally different world, and she couldn't blab to Aiden, not while Logan still wasn't sure she was ready to publicly come out.

"Well, I'm just glad we're hanging out tonight," Aiden said after a minute. "I've missed you."

"I missed you too, you sap." She smiled at him. "Let's go get Alexis and hit the town."

On the car ride, Aiden cranked up the volume, and hip-hop music thumped through the speakers.

"Have to get the party started early so we don't fizzle out," he yelled, as Alexis climbed into the back seat.

"You really are a nerd," she shouted back to him.

"You say that like it's a bad thing," he said, smiling at her. "Let's roll!" He put the car in gear and drove through the neighborhoods until he pulled onto Central Avenue.

Turning down the music, he looked from Carter to Alexis. "Nachos from Two Fools Tavern to start the night?" He glanced at the clock. "We can still get in for another couple of hours before they turn it to twenty-one and up."

Carter considered the options. If they grabbed dinner and headed back to Aiden's, they'd be sure to be home before people got too crazy. Her thoughts drifted to Logan, and she hoped she'd be safe and smart tonight.

Thinking back to the dance, she knew Logan wouldn't risk an unsafe ride home. If nothing else, she'd probably crash at Josie's. "Nachos sound great," she said, realizing they were both waiting for her as the deciding vote.

He pulled his car into the parking lot behind the building and reached his fist out for a fist bump. Obliging him, Carter pounded his fist.

After they were seated and served sodas, Aiden turned to them both. "So, it's our last semester of high school, what do you hope this next year brings?" He took a sip of his drink. "And none of the obvious things like 'graduate with honors,' or 'have a good time with my friends,'" he added.

"You're such a dad sometimes," Carter joked.

"She's right, you know?" Alexis said, shaking her head. "But I'll go first. I want to go skydiving the summer after we graduate."

"What? Really?" Aiden's eyes widened.

"Yeah, my parents offered to take me for something fun after graduation, and that's what I picked. I think it'll be wild."

"You probably win with the big announcements, unless Carter over here is going to tell us she wants to get a girlfriend, or actually ask someone out." He nudged Carter's chair, and she shook her head.

"Is getting a girlfriend really as groundbreaking as a skydiving announcement?" she countered.

"Could be." Aiden shrugged. "What do you want to do then?"

"I want to figure out where I'm going to college, for starters. Then I want to make some more memories with my mom."

"Those are all the obvious ones," Aiden protested.

Across from her, Alexis nodded. "Try again," she said, smiling as she toyed with her straw.

"Fine, I want to take a few more chances with things."

"What kind of things?" Aiden asked, leaning his elbows onto the table.

"All kinds of things. Art, maybe a love life one day, my writing. Just take a few risks." She thought about it for a second and nodded, satisfied with her answer.

"If you're looking to take a chance tonight, that girl over there two tables down has been eyeing you since we walked in," Alexis said, nodding her head to the left.

Carter didn't want to, but curiosity got the best of her, and she glanced in the girl's direction. A blonde in a flowing, paisley-print dress nodded in her direction when she looked. She nodded in return and cast her eyes back to Alexis.

"She's holding a beer. She's too old for me."

"You're eighteen," Aiden said, looking at the blonde and waving.

"Stop it," Carter said, kicking him under the table. "What is your problem?"

"Nothing. She's cute. That's all. She's cute, and she's into you. I told you that suit was going to be a lady killer tonight." He waved at her again, motioning for her to come join them.

"I'm not looking for anything like that tonight," she said, still feeling the blonde's eyes on her. "I really just want to hang out with my friends and have a nice, fun evening. Can we drop it?"

"We could," Alexis said, "but she's headed over here."

"I hate you," Carter said under her breath in Aiden's direction.

A second later, Carter felt the booth move slightly, as the blonde leaned up against her side of the table.

"I haven't seen you in here before," she said, looking at Carter. "I'm Kelly."

"Hi, Kelly," Aiden said, extending his hand and inserting himself into Kelly's line of sight. "This is my best friend, Carter."

"I'm perfectly capable of my own introductions," she said, casting him a glare. "Hi, Kelly."

"It's nice to meet you, Carter," she said, smiling as she glanced down at the soda on the table. "I'd offer to buy you a drink, but are you not drinking?"

"I'm in high school," Carter said, shaking her head.

"Oh, I see," Kelly said, taking a step backward. "Sorry about that." She nodded. "Have a fun evening."

With that, she turned on a heel and headed back to her table. Relieved, Carter looked from Aiden to Alexis. "Never do that to me again."

"I just waved," Aiden said, feigning innocence. "I was being friendly. Also, you didn't have to lead with the high school bit. She probably thinks you're underage, and that's why she got so creeped out."

"No," Carter corrected. "She got creeped out, because it's creepy for an adult to hit on a high school student. Why are you so obsessed with my dating life anyway?"

"I'm not." He crossed his arms over his chest. "I just want you to be happy."

"Then let me be here in the moment and be happy." As much as she tried to keep the edge out of her voice, she knew she was failing.

By the end of dinner, Aiden was pouting, and she was angry. His continual pressure on her to date was crossing a line, and she was over it.

"I'm going to go on home," she said once they were outside the restaurant.

"You can't," he said. "We have plans."

"You two go on without me. I'll be fine. I'd rather be at home."

"This is our last New Year's Eve before you move away," he said, throwing his hands up in the air.

"I'm sure I'll visit," she said, turning to walk away. She turned back. "I'll text you later," she promised. "I just want to do my own thing tonight."

"Whatever," he said, turning to Alexis. "Are you still down to party?"

Alexis nodded. She waved at Carter. Carter waved back. Alexis was nothing but a victim of the friendly fire warfare that was happening here.

"Do you want a ride home?" Aiden asked.

"I'll call an Uber," Carter said, waving behind her.

His stunt at the restaurant would have crossed a line any day, but tonight, it was just salt in the wound that she had someone but couldn't talk about it. With a sigh, she rounded the corner and pulled out her phone.

She had an unread text from Logan.

How's your night going?

She thought about how to respond, but didn't want to derail Logan's night. She could ask how the party was going. For a second, she leaned up against a building and thought about going to the party. Maybe it wouldn't be so bad. She'd get to see Logan in those leather pants, maybe let loose and dance to a couple of songs. She could blend in well enough.

Shaking her head, she stopped the thought process. Logan would be forced to face her friends. It wasn't a good fit.

Hey, it's fine. How's yours? She typed the reply and hit Send. Opening up the Uber app, she typed in her address and sighed. There was already a surcharge, making the price far higher than normal, but it would be worth it to get away from a situation she no longer wanted to be in.

Logan texted back. *It would be so much better if you were here. I know you're having a good time with your friends, but if you want to come by later, there are a lot of people. No one will even notice anything out of the ordinary.*

Are you sure? She replied.

OMG! Does that mean you're coming? Logan's reply came in almost instantaneously.

Had a fight with Aiden. I was going to head home, but if you want me there, I'll come there instead.

Yes! A million times yes. Despite her racing heart and mounting nerves, she smiled at Logan's exuberance. Logan sent over the address in a text. Taking a deep breath, Carter typed the address into the Uber app and called a car.

It might be a mistake, but as Wayne Gretzky had said, you missed one hundred percent of the shots you didn't take. She smiled at the thought. She'd take her shot and go spend the evening with her own superstar.

CHAPTER SIXTEEN

Dance music blared through the house, and Logan looked around the room, watching the madness unwind. She was still unsure how Josie's parents ever turned a blind eye to the chaos of the parties their daughter threw. They'd opted to travel to Mexico for an anniversary celebration, leaving Josie and her younger sister unsupervised on New Year's weekend.

Big mistake, Logan thought, looking from the keg in the kitchen to the dance party that had taken over the oversized living room. Thirty or forty high school kids crowded into the house, all drinking like they had sorrows to drown. She'd lost count of the guests an hour ago. Had she not seen it in person, she would have sworn this was the type of thing to only happen in movies.

She checked her phone once more, tapping the screen in anticipation. Carter should be here any minute.

"What are you doing, hiding out in here?" She heard Marco's voice, as he came to refill his cup.

"Just taking a breather," Logan said, laughing as she pointed to the dance floor. "Have to rehydrate between songs."

"I hear that," he said, taking a swig of his beer and holding the cup up to cheers her. "How've you been by the way? I haven't seen you since the dance."

"I've been good." She knew she shouldn't care, but she was being polite. "How's he holding up?"

"Do you really want to know?" Marco winced.

"I know he's got some new girlfriend already." Logan took a sip of her beer. "I'm happy for him. It's good to move on. I know Josie told him he wasn't invited tonight, but there's no chance he'll swing by unannounced, is there?"

Marco laughed. "He didn't take that too well, but I guess he and the new girlfriend are going to do something else. He said they'd be in Taos, so there's no chance of them stopping in."

"Good," she said, nodding. The last thing she needed was Barrett showing up to cause a scene.

"I'm sorry about all that stuff he said." Marco shook his head. "I know he's my best friend, but he can really be an ass sometimes. You didn't deserve all that."

"Thanks, Marco," she said, patting his shoulder. "You're one of the good ones." She looked around the room to find Josie. She smiled, watching her best friend do a line dance. "She deserves that, you know? One of the good ones. Don't mess it up."

"I wouldn't dream of it," he said, smiling as he walked past her to join Josie on the dance floor.

Her phone buzzed, and she pulled it out of her pocket, smiling as she saw Carter's name on the screen.

I'm here. Do I just walk in? Do I knock?

Logan headed for the door. She opened it quietly and stepped outside, finding Carter standing on the front porch with her hands shoved in her pockets.

She looked around and kept her voice low. "You look even better in person. Follow me." Making her way around the side of the house, she slipped into the garage and turned on the lights. Thankfully, it was deserted.

"Are you hiding me away?" Carter asked, laughing as she looked around.

"Not at all." Logan set her beer on a shelf and closed the distance between her and Carter. "I just wanted a second with you all to myself, before we go into the den of craziness."

"Oh yeah?" Carter's voice was low and sultry. "Why the alone time?"

"I think you know why," she said, grabbing the back of Carter's neck and pulling her in for a kiss. This time she wasn't soft and slow. She pressed Carter up against the wall and kissed her with passion.

As she leaned back, she shook her head. "God, I've been waiting to do that."

"This is the best party I've been to so far in high school," Carter said, giving her a thumbs-up. "Five stars."

"I'll have to make sure I keep that rating through the rest of the night," Logan said, laughing and leaning in for another quick kiss. "Thanks for coming by the way."

"It was either this, or slipping into my PJs and watching whatever washed-up singer they have performing on TV prior to the ball drop tonight. It was a tough choice," she said, smiling as she reached up to grab Logan's belt loop. "These pants might have sealed the deal though. I needed to see them in person."

Logan stepped back, delighting in the way Carter's eyes lit up, as she looked her up and down. She turned slowly in a full circle. "Do you like these?" she asked, laughing as she turned.

"Very much," Carter said, nodding.

"Grapes and leather pants." Logan laughed. "You're easy enough to please."

"Grapes and leather pants, like at the same time, might cause me to burst into flames on the spot." Carter sucked in a breath and nodded in approval.

"I might have to see what Josie has in her fridge."

"Tonight we'll behave," Carter said, shaking her head. "Aside from maybe another trip to the garage if it gets to be too much in there." She ran her finger back along the belt loop. At the simple touch, Logan tensed. "But you can wear these anytime."

She heard footsteps nearby and took a step back. Clearing her throat, she beckoned Carter to follow her. "Let's go inside," she suggested. As they made their way out the back door, she heard someone else open up the side door through which they'd entered.

"Sweet, it's empty." She heard a guy whose voice she couldn't place.

"Just in time," she whispered, pulling Carter from the garage and back up to the porch.

"Who all is in there?" Carter asked, once they were out of earshot, motioning to the house. "Anyone I actually know, so I won't be glued to your side the whole night."

Logan looked from side to side. She hadn't considered the thought, aside from getting Carter here. She'd only known she'd do her best to make sure Carter felt comfortable. "I think there's a handful of people you know or can at least make conversation with. It's not just the sports teams. Seriously, I'm not sure who invited half of these people."

"That's what they're going to say about me, you know?" Carter laughed.

Logan reached out, running her hands along Carter's arms. "It's not like that. I invited you. As best friend of the host, I get invitation privileges. For example, I got someone uninvited, simply by existing."

"Barrett?" Carter asked hopefully.

Logan nodded, smiling proudly. "He won't be anywhere near here tonight."

"That's a relief. I'm not worried about fitting in. I just don't want to take away from your time with your friends."

"If you're worried about it, you can invite Aiden and Alexis. I don't know what they're doing tonight."

Carter shook her head, her expression darkening. "I don't really want to mix the two worlds quite like that, not tonight."

"What happened?" Logan asked, reaching out to grab Carter's hand. She gently massaged her hand, before pulling away. It was too risky right here, especially after all of the rumors.

"He tried to set me up with some college girl."

"Did you tell the college girl you have a girlfriend?" As soon as the words escaped her mouth, she wished she could take them back.

"Do I have a girlfriend?" Carter smiled and raised an eyebrow.

"I mean." Logan laughed nervously. She gripped the beer cup and took a drink. "Do you want to have one? Sorry, I realize now I shouldn't have said that."

"If I have a girlfriend, she's cute and a little awkward, but otherwise the most confident person you'll ever meet," she said, her smile growing with each word.

"Does that mean…" Logan's voice trailed off, as she looked deep into Carter's eyes. "Are we?"

"Do you want to be my girlfriend?"

Logan smiled, and the door opened with Josie standing in the doorway.

"What are you two doing out here?" she asked, throwing her hands in the air. "Come inside. It's freezing."

Logan froze. How long had she been watching? Was she able to hear? She assessed the situation quickly. With the music streaming from the house, Logan was sure she was in the clear. "We were just catching up," she said, smiling at Josie. "I invited Carter to join us tonight." She looked in Carter's direction, nodding at her, hoping Carter knew she was answering the question that still lingered. "Carter, you remember Josie? Josie, Carter."

"Yeah, we've met a handful of times. Come in, Carter," she said, allowing Carter to go in first.

"What are you doing?" Josie asked quietly, leaning in to speak directly to Logan.

"Bringing my friends together," Logan said, shaking her head. "Hope it's cool." Not waiting for a response, she followed Carter into the kitchen.

Once inside, Logan nodded to the keg. "Would you like a drink?" she asked Carter.

Carter looked around the room, as if she was taking it all in. She waited a second and nodded slowly. Under Josie's watchful eye, Logan poured Carter a cup.

"Hey, Logan," Josie called out over the music. "Can you help me grab some things from the basement?"

Logan looked to Carter, careful to keep her voice low. "Are you good in here?"

"Go ahead," Carter said. "I know some of these people. I'll be fine."

"Coming," Logan said to Josie. She walked closely by Carter. "The answer is yes, by the way," she whispered in Carter's ear.

Carter smiled, pressing her beer to her lips to hide the gesture. "Good," she said quietly, before turning and heading toward the group of underclassmen at the game table.

Following Josie, Logan's head spun. She had a girlfriend. Just weeks ago, she'd had a long-term boyfriend, and no one questioned her sexuality, let alone her. Now, all she knew was that she came alive when Carter was around, and everyone was questioning what she was doing.

Down in the basement, Josie flipped on a light. "What is going on with you?" she asked, turning so they were face-to-face.

"I don't know what you mean."

"Yes, you do." Josie turned and started pacing. "First you two are friends all of the sudden, which is fine. That's cool. I'm not jealous. I know you're my best friend. But then, you're secretly inviting her to my party, after we went over the guest list together."

"I thought it would be fine," Logan said, shaking her head. "I'm sorry I didn't run it by you, but there are at least ten people here who weren't on the guest list."

"People bring plus ones," Josie said, putting her hand on her hip. "We didn't account for that, but it's fine. We have plenty of beer and food, and we've made sure no one is driving. We'll figure out enough room for everyone, so that we all stay safe."

"Then what's the problem?"

"It's just…" Josie shook her head and ran her fingers through her hair. "It's just that I don't know why you'd invite her here when there are already rumors going around that you're a…" She paused and looked down to the ground. "Look, since Barrett posted that photo, everyone has been talking. I've spared you from most of it, because I don't want you to be self-conscious, but people are talking a lot." She sighed. "It's not that they're saying all negative things. It's just that it's *you*. You're not a lesbian. You've been with Barrett all this time, and they can't stop talking about it. It's the shock value of it all. They want to know the juicy gossip, and right now, that's you. You're the talk of the town."

"I know that," Logan said, taking another drink. "I'm well aware that I'm the center of attention, yet again. If it's not because I have a dead brother and don't drive, it's because I broke up with my boyfriend."

"Why fuel the rumors, though? That's all I want to know. You could have easily had fun with your friends tonight, showed everyone that you're doing fine and not rebounding with some girl, and let things get back to normal." Josie's voice was rising with each word, and Logan felt her face warm with anger.

"Maybe I don't want things to get back to normal." Logan threw her hands up in the air, spilling beer on the carpet as she did so. "Normal was pretty shitty for me, okay?"

"And what? She makes it all better. Is that it?"

"Yeah," Logan admitted. "She does." She crossed her arms over her chest defensively and shook her head at Josie. "You won't get it, but she does."

"Are you two…" Josie trailed off, turning to pace some more. "Should I even ask it?"

"Depends on what you want to hear, I guess," Logan said, setting her cup on a shelf so she didn't spill more of it in her frustration. "If you want the truth, you don't have to ask for it. We're together. She's my girlfriend." She watched as Josie's eyes widened and her mouth fell open. Logan put her hands on her hips. "It is what it is, Josie. Sorry I didn't tell you sooner. I'm just figuring it all out."

"I just can't believe you never told me," Josie said, shaking her head. "We've been best friends forever. How do you keep that much of yourself a secret from someone who has shared everything with you?"

"I didn't know," Logan said. She grabbed her cup and drank the last sip. "I'm out of beer, and I really thought this conversation with you of all people would have been easier." She turned to walk up the stairs, but turned back halfway down. "You're the only one besides Ben I've told," she said quietly.

"I'm not going to say anything, if that's what you're worried about. I thought you knew me better than that." She huffed and put her hands on her hips. "But then again, I thought I knew you too."

Logan walked back up the stairs, fighting back tears with every step. Josie had no idea what she'd been through, the internal wrestling, the risks she was taking. She shook her head as she pushed open the door, almost hitting Marco on the way out.

"Have you seen Josie?" he asked, looking around. "I haven't been able to find her anywhere."

"She's down there." Logan pointed.

"Are you okay?" He stepped back and looked at her, frowning as he tried to read her expression.

"Never better," Logan lied. She moved past him and made her way to the kitchen. She glanced over the side of the room, where Carter was sinking a shot at beer pong.

"You're on fire," Justin, one of the football boys said, giving her a high five.

Logan leaned against the counter, pouring herself a water to cool off and watching the scene unfold. Within minutes, Carter had sunk every shot. She poured two more cups from the keg, and as the game wrapped up, she walked over to the table.

"Thought you weren't much of an athlete," she said quietly, handing Carter a freshly poured beer.

"You never asked about beer pong." She laughed. Stepping away from the table, she took a bow to appease the crowd that was asking her for another game. "Is everything okay with you two?" she asked when they were away from the group.

"I told her." Logan crossed her arms over her chest, still waiting for her blood to stop boiling. "She was the worst. Acted like the whole thing was some big secret I kept from her, when really I was just trying to figure it out."

"Not everyone gets that," Carter said, gently patting her on the shoulder. "I'm sure she'll come around. She doesn't strike me as the homophobe type."

"She's not. She never has been. I think it's all just too fresh."

"I'm here while she's figuring it out," Carter said. "I know that can be tough. In the meantime, do you want to stay?"

Logan looked around the house. For years, she'd felt as comfortable here as she did in the walls of her own home. Now, everything seemed off its axis. She nodded stubbornly. "Yes, I do. I helped decorate and plan the music for this party, and I'm going to enjoy it." Taking a deep breath, she reminded herself that these were her friends too, and she belonged as much as anyone else did.

"Want to dance?" Carter asked. She nodded in the direction of the dance floor, where everyone was moving to their own beats, the effects of the alcohol clearly starting to kick in for most of the partygoers.

She nodded. Dancing had always seemed to provide an escape from whatever was stressing her, and dancing with Carter was something she knew would lift her spirits in an instant.

"What's your plan after this, by the way?" Carter asked, stepping in between her and the dance floor. "Were you planning to stay here?"

"I was, but I don't think I want to anymore."

"I'll make sure you get home safe," Carter assured her.

"My dad isn't expecting me home." She looked at the floor. She'd never considered that she might be at odds with Josie, so she'd planned to stay over. "I don't want to wake him up. After the dance at school, I set off the house alarm, because he'd set it thinking I was going to be out all night. He was really cool about it, but I know he hasn't been sleeping, so waking him up really sucks."

"You can stay at my place if you need to," Carter said. She looked down at the floor. "We have a couch, and there's a guest room. Your pick."

"What if I pick somewhere else?" Logan smiled mischievously as her mind ran rampant with the possibilities.

Carter bit her lip, shaking her head. "I'd love that, but you've been drinking. I've been drinking."

"I've only had one, and I'm happy to stop," Logan said, setting her beer on the counter. "Besides, I don't need to get too crazy anyway."

"Enjoy yourself. Be young," Carter urged. "There's plenty of time for other things, remember? We're not going anywhere."

"Okay," Logan said, picking up her drink. "You're such a…" She paused. "I was going to say gentleman, but that doesn't fit. You're chivalrous."

Carter laughed and shook her head. "I'm just a decent human. That's the difference."

As they moved to the dance floor, Logan let the music take away her cares. By the third song, she was both breathless and relieved of her earlier anger.

"Do you want one more?" she asked, pointing to Carter's cup. Carter nodded, handing her the cup. She turned to follow, and Logan shook her head. "Stay and dance. I'll be right back."

In the kitchen, she stopped when she saw Josie making a beeline for her. Turning her back, she redirected from the keg to the fridge. She filled her cup with water and downed it, hoping Josie would take the hint.

"I'm sorry," she said, coming to stand in front of Logan. "I reacted like a jackass."

"You don't know what it's like," Logan said, her words barely above a whisper. Gripping the edge of the counter, she fought to keep her anger at bay.

"I don't"—Josie shook her head—"and I'm really sorry I made it about me."

"You know I wasn't lying to you on purpose, right?"

"I know. It took me a little bit to get on board and understand that." Josie shook her head. "I promise to be your number one supporter."

"Okay." Logan looked down at the floor and then walked over to refill the beers.

"And I am happy for you," Josie said, closing the distance between them. "She seems cool."

"You have no idea," Logan said, looking back to the dance floor. "She's amazing."

"Does she want to crash here with you?"

Logan almost dropped the cup. She set it on the table and shook her head. Looking back at the dance floor, she contemplated the idea. "I don't know," Logan answered after a moment. Carter was dancing and at ease, clearly over her jitters at the beginning of the night, but she wasn't sure this was her ideal spot to crash.

"She's welcome to," Josie said. "The two of you can have the guest room if you want it." She leveled her gaze with Logan. "And you and I can catch up on whatever you're comfortable telling me over lunch soon."

"I'm sorry I didn't tell you sooner," Logan said. She took a drink and looked at Josie. Her expression had softened, and her smile told Logan she was genuine in her support. She let out a sigh of relief. "I just wanted some time to figure it all out."

"I get that now." Josie shrugged. "I didn't at first, but I can only imagine what you've been going through. I'm serious about the details, though. I want to know everything."

"You'll get them," Logan said, laughing as she moved toward the dance floor to deliver Carter's beer.

"Do you have to go back home?" Logan asked, as she handed Carter the beer.

"What did you have in mind?" Carter smiled as she accepted the drink and took a sip.

Logan bit her lip. "I'm still debating if it's a good idea or not, but Josie said we can both crash here."

"Hmm." Carter took another drink and pulled out her phone. "Uber rates are insane. I could either ask my mom for a ride and you can crash on our couch, or…" She looked around the party. "Where would we sleep?"

"They have a couch as well," Logan said. "Or you could sleep in the guest room with me." She smiled and shook her head. "I'll sleep on the floor if you're more comfortable that way, or if you're okay with it, I'd love to spend the night with you in my arms."

Carter closed her eyes and pursed her lips together. Smiling, she nodded. She glanced at the clock on her phone. "It's eleven fifty-two. Do you want to do the countdown down here, or would you like to have a New Year's kiss?"

"Upstairs!" Logan said.

"Upstairs it is."

Logan turned and found Josie at the edge of the dance floor. "I'm pretty tired," Logan said. "I think I'm going to go up and go to bed."

Josie looked from Logan to Carter and smirked. "Happy New Year," she said, shaking her head with a laugh.

"Happy New Year," Logan said, "and thank you."

She could still hear Josie's laugh as she made her way quickly up the stairs with Carter following right behind. Once behind the closed door of the guest room, Logan locked the door and resisted the urge to throw Carter on the bed. Instead, she took her time, taking a drink of her beer. Carter took a seat on the edge of the bed, before setting down her beer and coming closer to Logan.

"You can still hear the music," she said, pointing to the floor. "Would you like to dance with me the way I'd like to dance with you?"

Logan raised an eyebrow. "And how would that be?"

"Here, let me show you," she said, wrapping her finger in Logan's belt loop and pulling her closer, so their bodies touched. Moving to the rhythm, Carter ground her hips against Logan's.

Remembering the first dance they'd shared at school, Logan turned so Carter was behind her and shimmied down her body. Moving with the beat, Carter waited until she'd returned to her standing position. With a spin, Carter brought Logan back in front of her and leaned in for a long, slow kiss.

From the floor below, Logan could hear the countdown, but she was already lost in Carter's kiss. As the crowd yelled out "Happy New Year," Logan leaned back and smiled at Carter.

"Happy New Year," she said, kissing Carter again.

"Happy New Year to you."

As Logan pulled away, she slipped out of her shoes and climbed into bed. "Come join me," she said, patting the spot next to her.

With a nod, Carter followed suit and climbed into bed next to Logan. Nestling up against her chest, Carter snuggled into Logan's arms. Below them, the party continued, but Logan was sure no one was having as happy a New Year as she was in that moment.

CHAPTER SEVENTEEN

The air felt somehow lighter, as Carter pulled her car into the parking lot for the first day back to school after the break. In the few days that had passed since New Year's Eve, her heart had been a flurry of emotion, but today, she'd get a chance to see Logan in person again and have a chance for a fresh start.

"New year, new me," she said, laughing as she checked her reflection before getting out of the car. She didn't really believe in a 'new me' mindset, but everything around her felt brand new. Never before had she been on her way to class, where she'd be sitting in the same room as her girlfriend. The word still felt strange and foreign, but in a way that delighted her.

"Good morning." She heard Logan's voice behind her.

Turning, she smiled.

"What are you doing out here? I figured you'd still be in practice." Carter looked around, finding none of the other team members around the parking lot.

"I hurried through my shower and getting ready process." Logan looked down at her green and gray baseball tee and fitted jeans. She blushed. "I guess I maybe should have taken more time, looking at you now." She gestured to Carter, who was dressed in a sleek black button-down, tan pants, and ankle boots.

"Don't," Carter said, shaking her head. "You look amazing."

"Anyway…" Logan looked down at her feet. "I just wanted to say 'good morning' and walk with you to the school. Is that okay with you?"

"I'd love nothing more." Carter moved to take her hand, but pulled back. "Sorry," she said, biting her lip. "I guess habits form quickly."

"It's okay." Logan smiled. "Please don't apologize for wanting to touch me," she said quietly. "Soon," she added, falling into step beside Carter.

"This is good too." Even though holding hands or making contact was off-limits for the time being, simply getting to walk into the school together, getting to steal a couple of private moments was everything she could have hoped for.

"What are you doing after school?"

Carter checked her phone. "I'm supposed to hang out with Aiden. Nothing major, just smoothing things over after New Year's Eve."

"Have you talked to him since?"

"Yeah, we had it out the next day." Carter sighed. "Everything is fine. He had his feelings hurt that I left. I explained why I did what I did, and I think we're on the same page now."

"You can tell him, you know?" Logan stopped her approach to the school and turned to face Carter. "I told Josie. You trust him. Trust him with this and let him in."

"You sure?"

Logan nodded. "It's kind of on a need-to-know basis until I figure out how to tell my family, but I think your best friend needs to know. The last thing I want to do is come between you and people you care about."

Taking a deep breath, Carter nodded. "Okay, I'll tell him." She leaned back, considering a possibility. "Why'd you ask? What do you have planned this afternoon?"

"After practice, I was going to see if you wanted to grab a bite to eat. But since you have plans, I'll gladly accept a rain check."

"What would you say to me hanging out with Aiden while you're in practice, and then the three of us hanging out?" She bit her lip, hoping it wasn't too much of an ask. They'd hung out in crowds, but somehow hanging out with her best friend one-on-one felt more of a 'next step' kind of move.

Logan pressed her lips together and nodded slowly. "I think I could get on board with that," she said after a moment. "I mean, I kind of owe you after throwing you to the wolves at Josie's the other night."

"Want me to pick you up?"

"That would be great. Seven?"

"Seven it is." Carter smiled. "Now, go on in there and have a great day. I'll see you in class."

Logan waited a moment, as though she might protest. But she just moved her head to the side and nodded. "I was going to argue, but you're right. I'll see you in there." For a second longer, she paused, looking Carter up and down, her grin widening as she focused in on Carter's eyes. "You have a great day too," she called before turning and heading into the building.

This was going to be harder than Carter thought. Acting normal, when all she wanted to do was be close to Logan, was going to make for a long day—or better yet, a long semester.

"Hey stranger," Aiden called, running up behind her. "Are we okay?"

She turned to face him, and pulled him into a warm hug. "We're fine. I know I said it via text, but I'm sorry I left. I needed my space to deal with some things."

"Are you better now?"

"Much," she said with a nod. "Are we still on for after school?"

"I don't have any other plans." Aiden gave her an exaggerated shrug. He looked down at his watch. "We're going to be late."

As they zipped through the halls, grabbed books from their lockers and headed for first period, she glanced over to see Logan walking to class with Josie right by her side. From a distance, they shared a knowing look, before she quickly turned her attention back to Aiden. Luckily for her, he'd missed the whole thing while fumbling with his books.

"Did these things get heavier, or do I just really need to work out more?"

She laughed, helping him grab the falling stack. "You might want to hit the gym," she teased.

The morning passed in a blur of new assignments and class-wide lectures from teachers on not forgetting things they'd already covered. By the time lunch rolled around, Carter's head was spinning with a to-do list that already felt insurmountable.

"So much for easing us back into things, am I right?" Aiden said, sliding into the cafeteria table beside her.

"No joke. I already need a nap."

"That's something old people say," Aiden joked, unwrapping his sandwich and shaking his head.

"Old people and people who haven't been getting enough sleep."

"Oh?" His eyebrow shot up, and he stared at her in question, stopping his sandwich halfway to his mouth. Taking a bite, he shook his head. "Never mind. Forget I asked."

"It's okay," Carter said, shaking her head. "You don't have to be cautious around me. Just don't try to set me up with anyone else, and we'll be good."

He nodded, chewing. His scrunched-up expression was the same he wore when trying to figure out a math problem. She laughed. "Really, it's fine."

"Well then, why haven't you been sleeping?" He eyed her cautiously, as though she might get mad at him again.

"I've had a lot on my mind," she said.

"Cryptic."

She took a deep breath and grabbed the apple from her lunch. Taking a bite, she bought a second of normalcy. Once he knew, it was real. Not that it *wasn't* real. It had just felt like it was hers and only hers, and there had been something special about that too. Beside her, he looked like he might actually combust from curiosity.

It was time.

"There's a girl," she said slowly.

"I knew it." He smiled smugly. "Tell me more."

"You can't say anything."

"Who do I talk to?" He looked around the room, shaking his head at each face he saw. "Literally none of these people. If it's not you or Alexis, I barely say anything. And even if I do, it's not like they hear me."

"Except when you've had a little bit of spiked punch and start dancing with pretty girls," she reminded him.

"Yeah, but I didn't talk to her about you."

"Fair enough." She picked up her apple again, but stopped short of taking a bite. "I'll tell you all about her this afternoon. Just don't try to set me up. I'm already taken." With that, she turned her attention to her lunch.

"You can't just say that and leave it."

"This afternoon, you'll know everything, and then she'd like to join us for dinner, if you're okay with it."

Aiden leaned back and nodded so quickly he looked like a bobblehead. "Yeah, I get to hear all about the girl and then meet her? Of course I'm down. I have to see if she's good enough for my best friend anyway."

"She is," Carter said. "Promise." A slow smile spread over her face, and she blushed. "She's really good to me and for me." She took a sip of her water and leveled her gaze. "I'm very happy."

"If I would have known all of this on New Year's Eve…"

She held up her hand to stop him from talking. "Let's let New Year's Eve stay in the past. I think we both know we were a little dramatic, but let's go ahead and let it lie. Deal?"

He pressed his lips together, clearly holding back what he really wanted to say, but nodded. "Deal," he agreed.

From across the room, Alexis came storming over to their table. She stood in front of Carter with her eyes wide and a look that should have been reserved for people who'd lost someone or something they loved. "How are you holding up?"

"What are you talking about?" Carter placed her apple back on her tray, a knot forming in her stomach as Alexis looked down to the floor.

"You haven't heard?"

"Heard what?" She stood and walked over to comfort Alexis, even though she had no idea for what. "What's going on?"

"The newspaper office," Alexis said, shaking her head. "It's... it's wrecked."

"What?"

Alexis opened her mouth to speak but shut it just as quickly.

"I'll go check it out." She gathered her things and tossed her uneaten lunch in the trash, making her way down the hallway until she was greeted with shattered glass in front of the door to the small room, where the window had been broken out of the doorframe. Her heart pounded and she felt the heat of anger rush to her cheeks.

Stepping over the glass, she reached cautiously for the door handle. She stepped inside, flipped on the lights and looked around the room. Crumpled papers littered the floor, and her keyboard had been ripped from her computer and smashed against the wall. But worst of all, her prized possession—her camera—had been thrown to the ground. She picked it up carefully and examined its cracked lens.

Sliding down the wall, she sat with her camera in her hand. It hadn't been much, but this had been a project she'd fought for from the beginning, and now it felt as if she'd been violated. Even though they were just things, someone had taken the time out of their day to come into her space and destroy the things that had been hers. It was targeted, and that was disconcerting. Clutching her camera to her chest, she thought back to how she'd had to beg the school board for funding to purchase the equipment—even though she'd found it used and at a great price.

The sound of footsteps in the hallway jolted her to a standing position. Her heart pounding, she looked to the doorway.

"You startled me," she said, softening as she saw Logan standing there.

"This is awful." Logan walked over to pull Carter into her arms. "Who would have done a thing like this?"

Carter's heart pounded as she leaned into the embrace, a mix of anger, sadness, and fear still raging within her. She shook her head. Her emotions were still in control over her logic. She hadn't had a chance to think through possible culprits in the midst of her heartache.

Logan stiffened and pulled back, raw anger shining in her eyes. "That bastard," she said, shaking her head. She stepped back and placed her arms over her chest.

"Who? What?"

"Barrett." The name sizzled off Logan's tongue like a hiss. "He can mess with me all he wants, but you…this," she said, gesturing around the room, "it's off-limits. I'm going to make sure he pays for this." She turned on a heel, marching out the door.

"Wait," Carter said, holding up her hands. Seeing Logan's anger pulled her back into the reality of the situation. "I'll go with you. This isn't your fight."

"It is now," Logan said, softening her tone. "You're involved, and that makes it mine." She pulled Carter close to her again. Around them, a small crowd had gathered to check out the damage, the news of which had no doubt been spread around the cafeteria. Word traveled quickly in these halls, but Logan didn't seem to care about the crowd. Holding her tighter, Logan ignored the onlookers and kept eye contact with Carter. "I'm here in this with you. Let's go." Putting her arm around Carter's waist, Logan turned and walked, leading Carter to the principal's office.

Once outside of Dr. Rumble's office, Carter's heart raced. As Logan knocked on the locked door, Carter leaned up against the wall, working to catch her breath. When he didn't answer the door, Logan walked over to her. Placing her hands on Carter's arm for support, she leaned down to eye level.

"What can I do for you?" Logan asked gently.

The simple kindness in the words caused Carter to bite her lip, afraid she'd cry all over again. Shaking her head, she took a steadying breath. "I'll be okay." She stood upright and nodded at Logan. "Thank you for trying."

"I'm not giving up," Logan said, shaking her head. "I'm going to Susan's office next. I know he's in there. He's just avoiding students. He does it all the time. Come on."

Logan looped her arm through Carter's, offering silent encouragement, as she made the way to Susan's office, whose door was wide open.

"Logan," Susan called out. "It's been a while. Come in!" She stopped, no doubt in response to the scowl on Logan's face. "Oh, what seems to be the problem?" she asked, lowering her voice, as Carter and Logan stepped into the office.

"We need to see Rumble."

"What?" Susan looked over to the closed door. "Don't you usually avoid that?"

"It's important, and he's not answering his door." Logan's tone was pointed but respectful. "Can you please get him for me?"

Susan pursed her lips and folded her hands in her lap. For a moment, it looked like she might protest. She looked from Logan to Carter and back again before nodding. "Sure thing."

She walked over and knocked gently on the door.

Carter could hear the movement in his office and shook her head. He'd really been avoiding them, just as Logan had said.

When the door opened, he frowned at Susan, and then straightened as he realized she wasn't alone in the room.

"Girls," he said, acknowledging Logan and Carter with a nod. "What's going on in here?" He stepped into Susan's office and stared at them from the corner of the room.

"Barrett Swanson vandalized the newspaper office and destroyed school property," Logan said, her anger still ringing with each word. "He damaged a camera that belongs to the newspaper office, as well as computer equipment and a window and tore up god knows what else."

"Your boyfriend did this?" Dr. Rumble laughed and shook his head. "Why are you in here tattling on him?"

Logan leaned back as if she'd been slapped, and Carter's feelings of unease turned to anger. "He's not my boyfriend," Logan said. "Not anymore. But even if he was, I'd be in here telling you what he did, because it's wrong."

"This sounds like some kind of lovers' quarrel to me." Dr. Rumble shook his head. "You said there's damage?"

"Not a lovers' quarrel." Logan shook her head. "Look at this." She grabbed the camera from Carter's hands and thrust it into Rumble's. "If you want to walk down and see the rest, that would be great." She gestured to Carter who stood by her side. "Carter here has spent her entire high school career building that program from the ground up, creating a newspaper that people love to read, that keeps us all informed, and that showcases announcements from you even. She built a program that gives students hands-on experience before college." She paused and took a step back, taking a deep breath, clearly trying to calm herself down from the anger that raged inside her. She put her hands on her hips. "The fact of the matter is that he damaged a lot of things, but he also created an unsafe environment and it was a direct and targeted threat—not only to the property but also to Carter's safety and wellbeing."

"We'll replace your camera," Dr. Rumble said, handing it back over to Carter. "And I'll check with the janitorial staff about cleaning up the rest." He turned back to Logan. "What makes you so sure it was Barrett, if this isn't some sort of breakup vendetta?"

Logan's body was as stiff as Carter had ever seen it, and it looked as if Logan might actually lunge over the desk and sock him. He'd deserve it, but it would serve no purpose. Carter reached out, placing a reassuring hand on Logan's arm to ground her from her anger. Logan took a deep breath.

"He's never been good under pressure," Logan said after a moment. "He's also not smart enough to cover his tracks. Ask him, and I'll guarantee you'll have an answer." She glanced at the camera. "Even better than that, you won't have to pay for this," she said, pointing. "He will, saving the school money that's needed in other areas."

Rumble leaned back and nodded. His expression never changed from the frown he wore so often.

"He did it," Logan said once more, driving the point home. "And if nothing is done about it, he'll continue to escalate." She looked down at the floor. "This isn't his first move like this."

"What else are you insinuating?"

"Nothing that matters here at school," Logan said quietly. "But he's been on the attack against Carter for a while."

"Why's that?"

"He just has. Promise me you'll question him."

Rumble looked like he might protest again, but reluctantly nodded his head. "I will."

Logan didn't budge.

"You have my word," he reassured her.

Nodding, Logan looked to Susan. "Thank you."

Reaching for Carter's arm, Logan strode out of the office.

"You didn't have to do all that," Carter said, once they were back in the hallway. "But thank you."

"I probably should have let you speak." Logan leaned against the wall. "I'm sorry. I just got so carried away. What if he'd decided to hurt you instead of just things?"

"Don't apologize." Carter's heart was still pounding, and her voice was shaky. She was supposed to head back to the newspaper office, but now didn't want to be anywhere around the school.

"You should go rest up," Logan said, as if reading her mind. "Wait here, I'll be right back."

With that, she turned and walked back into the office, where Carter could hear Dr. Rumble and Susan arguing.

"I'm taking the next two periods off," Logan announced.

The confidence and strength she was displaying was admirable. Carter shook her head. She would have asked for them to do something and given an impassioned plea, but Logan wasn't taking 'no' for an answer.

"Why would you be skipping your studies?" Rumble's voice boomed out into the hallway. Carter had to wonder if anyone ever had any privacy at this place.

"I'm not," Logan said. "I'll make it all up, after practice if I have to, later this week. I just need to make sure she gets home safely. You can call my parents or her mom if you'd like, but I'm going to go do what's right." Her voice got quieter, and Carter couldn't make out what was being said, but after a moment, Logan returned.

She looked to the floor, taking a series of steadying breaths, and when she looked up, she was somehow calmer, more at ease. The anger that had flashed in her eyes still lurked somewhere below the surface, but in its place was a resiliency that made Carter lean back in awe.

"I'm taking you home. Give me your keys."

Carter shook her head. "It's okay. I'll drive."

"No," Logan said, pulling her into her arms. "I've got this. For you."

A million questions circled in her mind, but Carter reached into her pocket and pulled out the keys, handing them over to Logan. As they walked to the car, Logan never removed her arm from Carter's.

After opening the passenger door and insisting Carter get inside, Logan climbed into the driver's side and started the car.

"You don't have to do this," Carter said, placing a hand on Logan's leg.

"I do, actually." Logan turned to Carter with a nervous smile. Connecting her phone to the auxiliary cord, she queued up the music. "Seems like a good time for the playlist I made for you."

"You made me a playlist?" The tears Carter was holding back pooled in her eyes. She wiped them away, not wanting to seem overly dramatic.

"I did." Logan reached over and squeezed Carter's hand, as Joan Jett's voice filled the speakers.

She flipped down the visor mirror, smiling at her reflection with a decisive nod, as if she'd checked herself just enough to know she was ready. She put the car in gear, and Carter gave her directions. Logan gripped the steering wheel and set her jaw. Carter wanted to offer her support, but looked out the window, knowing that speaking now might hinder the huge step Logan was taking. On the drive, she smiled as Logan settled back into the driver's seat. By the time they pulled into her driveway, Logan looked at ease.

"Let's get you inside," she said, turning to offer Carter a sweet smile.

"That was pretty amazing, what you just did," Carter said, not budging from her seat. "I'm proud of you."

"Thank you." Logan swallowed and looked around the car. "It felt good." She took a deep breath and nodded. "Are you okay?"

"I am." Carter opened the passenger door and stepped from the car. "I probably shouldn't have taken the day, but I just didn't want to be there anymore. It seems like he really *hates* me."

"He's a bully," Logan said softly. "We'll face those demons tomorrow." Logan grabbed her hand, as Carter led the way to the front door. "For now, we can relax for a bit."

"You're staying?"

"For a while," Logan said, following Carter inside. "I want to make sure you're okay, and truthfully, I need to calm down before I go back. I haven't been that angry in a long time."

"I've never seen you like that," Carter agreed.

Logan glanced down at the floor and shrugged. "Sorry about that. I have a hot temper sometimes. It takes a lot to get it as bad as it was today, but when the floodgates open, it's hard to shut them."

"Please don't apologize," Carter said, feeling more at ease in her own home. She closed the distance between them and planted a kiss on Logan's lips. "You came to my rescue, demanded justice and refused to let anything—not Rumble, not driving a car, not classes—stand in your way." She kissed her long and slow this time. "I'm impressed."

"I probably won't be spearheading any fights in the near future, but I just might have to find other ways to impress you, if this is how you respond," Logan said, pushing Carter up against the wall and deepening the kiss. Carter wrapped her arms around Logan's neck, tangling her hands in her hair and pulling her closer.

"Carter? Is that you?" She jumped at the sound of her mom's voice. Looking up, she saw her mom laughing from the doorway of the kitchen. "Sorry," she said, looking away.

Logan stiffened and stepped backward, toward the door. "So sorry," she mumbled, her face reddening more with each passing second.

"Don't be sorry." Carter's mom stepped forward. "I'm Annie," she said, extending a hand. "I know we met briefly in the car the other night, but it's good to see you again."

Logan kept her eyes glued to the floor but reached out and shook her hand. "Nice to...um...see you."

"Welcome to our home," she said. She glanced at Carter, and Carter offered a nervous smile. This wasn't at all how they were supposed to hang out. She glanced down at the floor, then back to Logan and back to her mom.

"I was just leaving," Logan said.

"No you weren't," her mom said, waving for Logan to come inside. "What brings you two over here during the school day?"

Carter had to appreciate her mom, not automatically assuming they were skipping class, but then again, she knew her daughter better than that.

Logan, who had been so impassioned with the story earlier, now sat silently and looked at Carter.

Carter stifled a laugh. "It was a really bad day, Mom," she said, following her into the kitchen and practically dragging Logan along with her. "The newspaper office was vandalized, and Logan brought me home. I was pretty shaken up." Carter stopped and looked around the kitchen. "What are you doing home?"

"I only had a half-day schedule today, remember?" Her mom laughed. "Obviously you didn't, but that's fine. Have you both eaten?"

"I actually didn't." Carter reached to the top of the fridge to grab a bag of chips.

"Logan?" Carter's mom turned and extended the offer. Logan shook her head quickly.

"No thank you," she said, still shaking her head. "I'm fine."

"Have a seat," her mom urged. "I'll make some tea."

Beside her, Logan carefully sat, making sure to inch the chair further away from Carter than it was originally placed. Carter covered her mouth to quiet a laugh. She pulled out her phone and typed out a quick message.

It's fine. My mom is cool. Embarrassing? Sure. End of the world? No. She's not going to lecture us on anything.

She watched as Logan read her message and nodded, looking no more at ease than she had when they had first been caught. Logan slipped her phone back into her pocket and looked around the room.

"Thank you, Logan," her mom said, placing a cup of tea in front of her. "I really appreciate you being there to help Carter out today."

"Yes, ma'am," Logan said, smiling and staring into the teacup. "Thank you."

Her mom took a seat directly across from Logan. She took a sip of her own tea and smiled. "You don't have to be embarrassed," she said slowly, as if choosing her words carefully. "I'm really glad to see you, and I'm glad you're here."

"Thank you." Logan lifted the tea to her lips and took a small sip. "I'm glad to be here too. Thanks for having me."

"Carter tells me you play basketball. How's the season going?"

As if the cloud of awkwardness had been lifted an inch, Logan smiled and took a deep breath. "It's going well, thank you for asking."

Still in 'impress the parents' mode, but now leaning back in her chair and looking a bit more relaxed, Logan filled Carter's mom in on some of the highlights of the season thus far and the upcoming games.

Carter smiled. This was *almost* how she'd envisioned their first introduction. She knew she'd have a conversation coming with her mother about the day's events, but for the moment, she embraced the comfort of having her mom and Logan in the same room, chatting over tea.

CHAPTER EIGHTEEN

The cold wind whipped around her face, but Logan stayed leaned up against the side of Josie's car for another minute.

"Tell me again how you got caught," Josie teased, her laughter ringing out in the cool night air.

Logan shook her head and looked down at the ground. "Then her mom just offered me tea and sat and talked with me about basketball, like I hadn't been in the middle of kissing her daughter against a wall." She let out a nervous laugh. "I'm still not over it."

"Talk about an iconic meet the parents story." Josie shoved her hands in her pockets. "I hope you two get married, so she can tell the story at the reception."

"Oh god!" Logan buried her face in her hands. "I'm never going to live this down, am I?" She paused, replaying Josie's words. "Also, it's a little soon to talk about all that."

"Well, it's not too soon for *me* to talk about it." Josie laughed. "It would be weird if you did, I guess. Aside from making out in front of her mom, how's that going?"

Logan bit her lip, unable to contain her smile. "It's so crazy and so good." She looked around the parking lot, where some of her teammates still filed out of the parking lot. "Let's get in your car, and I'll tell you more."

"Yes, details!" Josie pumped her fist into the air, unlocking the car. "Text Ben and tell him I'm taking you home tonight. You can fill me in on the drive, and then you can get back to your hot date."

"Not so much of a hot date tonight, I'm afraid," Logan said, pulling out her phone to send a text over to Ben. Fortunately, his practice had run later than hers today, which meant she had a little bit of time to chat with Josie and to decompress after the afternoon's whirlwind of events. She'd gone from pissed off to victorious to turned-on to mortified in a matter of minutes, and even after a grueling practice, she hadn't settled back into normal mode.

As she climbed into the car, she winced. The pain in her shoulder was only getting worse. Hiding her face from Josie, she popped a couple of over-the-counter pain relievers from her bag and swallowed them. She'd ignored it as best she could since the accident, and she was convinced if she could hold on just a little longer, she could get through the season without it causing even more problems.

"Now that we're alone, tell me more." Josie's eyes sparkled with delight, as she turned down the music.

"It's like I finally get it," Logan said. She shrugged, trying to find the right words. She looked out toward the snow-covered mountains, remembering the night she'd held Carter's body so close to her own down by the foothills. She cleared her throat. "I get what it is to actually want someone, to like them, to crave their touch."

"Oh, girl," Josie said, shaking her head, "you've got it bad."

"I do," Logan admitted. She shoved her hands in her pockets and smiled at Josie. "But I'm not afraid of that. I always kind of thought I would be, like, to really feel something. With Barrett, it just wasn't there." She glanced down at the floorboard. "I guess those reasons are a little clearer now."

"Yeah? About that." Josie put the car in gear and backed out of her parking space. "I know it wasn't there with him, but is it just girls that do it for you? Are you bi, or lesbian, or what?"

"I don't really know." Logan considered the question. "I've never really felt anything for any of the guys. I'd laugh and joke with you all about who was attractive, because that's all we ever talk about." She laughed. "Not everyone is boy crazy, like you."

"Clearly." Josie laughed. "But not all of us have a hot, trendy librarian to give us our sexual awakening either."

"You think she's hot?"

"She's gorgeous, and has that super smart look," Josie said. She raised an eyebrow at Logan. "Like, she looks like she could take on the world, make me a kickass latte, write a book I'd like to read, and make me want to raid her closet, all at the same time."

"She can do all of that," Logan said, smiling. "But for me, she does a whole lot more."

"More?" Josie laughed. "Has there been more?"

Logan shook her head. "Not yet."

Josie tilted her head to the side in question.

"Eventually, I'm sure. If she keeps kissing me the way she does, it's inevitable." Logan sighed, leaning her head back into the seat. "I want to though. That's the difference. I never wanted to before."

"That's good. You know, you look a whole lot happier these days."

"Thank you." Logan basked in the compliment. "I feel happier. And it's not just about sex, you know? I mean, I get it. I have the raging hormones, same as everyone else, but even not kissing her, not having sex, just hanging out, it's pretty amazing. We talk about things. We listen to music. She makes me feel so special."

"I never want to be one of those insensitive girls who says that dating girls must be so much easier," Josie said, shaking her head, "but you really put the sell on it. I'm glad you have something so amazing."

"You do too," Logan said, waving her hand through the air. "I think you lucked out with Marco."

"He's all right," Josie said, laughing as she ran her fingers through her hair. "I'm kidding," she added. "I guess we're both pretty lucky. By the way, I got a text from him as we were leaving practice. Your talk with Rumble paid off."

"What happened?" The day had been so full of events, she'd forgotten to even ask.

"Barrett confessed to the whole thing. Rumble finally stepped up and made him bargain so he didn't get suspended. He's paying for a brand-new camera, and to fix all of the damage. He's also in after-school classes for the rest of the month and on a probationary period. If he has even the slightest slip up, he'll be suspended and risk losing his scholarship."

"Couldn't have happened to a nicer guy," Logan said dryly.

"So what are you doing tonight?" Josie asked, as she pulled into Logan's driveway.

"I'm hanging out with Carter and her best friend." Logan laughed, bringing the day full circle. "Already hung out with her mom, so I guess I'm knocking it all out in one day."

"Just be yourself, and it'll be fine." Josie wrapped her in a hug. "Besides, I'm sure her best friend won't mind if you make out with her."

"Stop," Logan said, laughing as she gathered her things to exit the car. "I'll let you know how it goes."

"I'll be waiting," Josie said, waving before pulling out of the drive.

Thankful to have the house to herself, Logan dressed quickly. Carter would be arriving in about fifteen minutes, giving her just enough time to freshen up and change clothes. As she dressed, she cranked up the playlist she'd made for Carter. Canadian pop singer, Adaline, streamed through her speaker, singing of crossing the line, and Logan shook her head, replaying this afternoon in her mind. Carter had recommended her music, and Logan couldn't get enough, but the song was a little on the nose for the situation. There was no way she was ever going to be able to face Annie without blushing, she was certain.

Taking a look in the mirror, she nodded. Simple but fashionable, a red sweater and ripped jeans. Nothing that should set either of them into a hormone-fueled frenzy the way her leather pants had. Reaching into her closet, she ran her fingers across the fabric of the pants that had fueled the lust-filled fire in Carter's eyes.

"Soon," she whispered with a low laugh. She'd break them out again, when Carter least expected it, just to see that look in her eyes again. But tonight wasn't the night. They'd already crossed one boundary for the day, and that was enough.

As Carter's car pulled into her drive, she bounded down the steps. She took a deep breath. Tonight would be fine. It had to be easier than it had been meeting Annie. She'd seen Aiden around school and even talked to him a time or two. He was a nice guy.

"Hop in," Aiden called out, exiting the front seat and climbing into the back seat.

"I can sit back there," she offered, but he shook his head, already fastening the seatbelt.

"Congrats, by the way," he said as she climbed in. "I know I'm sworn to secrecy, but I'm happy for the two of you."

"Thanks," she said, giving him a nod, before turning her attention to Carter.

"Hey," Carter said, smiling as she pulled out of the driveway.

Logan flashed her a smile, thankful for the music that played from the speakers.

"Did you want to put your playlist back on?" Carter offered.

Logan's cheeks got hot and she shook her head, remembering the song that was playing when she left the house. It was more suited for Carter's ears alone.

"Okay," Carter laughed, taking her silence for an answer. "Are you hungry for anything in particular?"

"Pizza," Aiden called out over the music.

"Pizza's good," Logan agreed.

As they got out of the car and piled into a booth at a spot near downtown, Aiden pulled off his coat and leveled his gaze at Logan. "I want to know everything." He spread his hands out on the table.

Logan laughed, looking at the menu to buy a minute. "About what?" she asked after a pause.

"About you. How long have you known?"

Carter kicked him under the table, and Logan laughed. "It's fine," she said, waving in Carter's direction. "I'll indulge it a bit." She turned her attention to Aiden. "Your beautiful best friend was an eye-opener for me." She glanced over at Carter. "She's pretty special, you know?"

"Dammit." Aiden shook his head. "First off, that's super cute, but also, kind of ew. But, second of all, I was supposed to give you the 'be good to her or else' conversation, and you took the wind out of my sails with all that cheesy stuff."

"Speaking of cheesy stuff," Carter said, changing the topic of conversation. "How about some cheesy bread to start, and then the veggie pizza with green chile?"

"Can we get half with bacon?" Aiden asked, smiling broadly.

"I like him already," Logan said, smiling at Carter and then at Aiden.

As they ate, Logan was thankful Aiden slowed his interrogation down, and by the time dinner was finished, she felt more confident that their two worlds could blend nicely.

"You running with a new crew, Watts?" Logan turned at the sound of her name. Brad Keller, a junior who played football with Barrett, stood in front of their booth.

"Hi, Brad," she said. She knew the smile on her face was fake, but didn't care to change it. "Just having dinner with some friends."

Brad looked from Logan to Carter and back again. "Looks like Barrett might not have been too off-base, huh?"

"Have a good night, Brad," she said, laying money down on the table to cover the bill before standing. "Have to get home and study."

"I don't care." Brad took a step back to get out of her way. "I think it's hot."

"That's enough," Aiden said, coming between Brad and Logan.

"Oh, you brought along a tough guy?" Brad asked, laughing and looking at Aiden. "Don't." Brad bowed up his chest in a ridiculous display of showing off his muscular frame.

"Let's go." Logan grabbed Aiden's arm and pulled him behind her and Carter. "Brad, again, have a good night."

Back in the car, Aiden was fuming. "The nerve of that guy," he said, smacking the seat next to him.

"Brad wasn't always an asshole," Logan said, shaking her head. "It's sad that he's turned into one, but it seems like that's what happens when we shove them all in a weight room. They just talk to one another and get stupider as a collective, focused on nothing but tough guy displays and testosterone."

"That sounds kind of homoerotic," Aiden said. "But still, he shouldn't be able to talk to you like that."

"If I didn't like you before, I like you even more now," Logan said to Aiden with a smile, as she reached over and grabbed Carter's hand. "Next time, what do you say we order in, and we can play that video game Carter said you liked?"

"That video game?" Aiden laughed, breaking up the tension in the car. "Has she seriously never played Mario Kart?" He looked at Carter, then back to Logan. "Your dating life is sadder than I thought," he said to Carter.

Carter laughed. "We've been kind of busy with other things, outside of the basement. But I'd be down for a Mario Kart night." She looked to Logan. "What do you think?"

As long as it didn't involve Brad, Barrett, or any of the other jerks they ran with, she'd be happy. For a city, sometimes Albuquerque felt like a tiny town. She nodded. "I'm in." She turned to Aiden. "On one condition."

"I'm not letting you win, and neither will she," Aiden said, shaking his head matter-of-factly.

"I don't want to win unless it's a fair fought victory, but if I'm going to explore your world, you're going to explore mine. Basketball game tomorrow night. Will you be there?"

"I can do that," he said after a moment of contemplation. "We all know Carter will be going anyway, so I'll have someone to sit with."

"Perfect." There had really been no reason to bargain. She would gladly enjoy a night of video games and hanging out at home, but as Carter's closest friend, she wanted him to feel like he was still a part of her life. She thought back to how many friendships she'd seen ruined when someone started dating someone new. She wasn't going to be the cause of that.

* * *

At the start of the third quarter, the Cougars led by six. Logan stretched her neck to the side, hoping it would ease up some of the pain in her shoulder. They'd known the game against Santa Fe High was going to be tough, but she hadn't expected it to be this physical. She was sure she was going to be covered in bruises by the end of the night, with both teams ending the first half in the foul bonus.

When the ref blew his whistle, she settled into her position on the defensive side of the court. Watching the player she was guarding, she adjusted her position and bent her knees in anticipation. As the ball was thrown her way, Logan readied herself. Eyes on the stomach, no easy shots. With a hand in her face, she saw the offensive player lean to drive to the basket. Planting herself firmly in front, she took the charge. At the initial contact, she saw red. She heard the pop. By the time her head whipped back and she lay on the court, fresh pain stung her right side.

She didn't hear the whistle over the searing pain she felt. Around her, Josie leaned down, offering a hand up. Logan moved to lift her right arm. Wincing, she bit down hard on her tongue so she didn't scream. She tasted blood. Chiding herself, she offered her left hand up to Josie, who pulled her upright.

"Are you okay?" Josie asked. Her brows were knit together tighter than Logan had ever seen. She nodded and tried to rotate her shoulder, but the stabbing pain stopped her.

"I think I need a sub," she said to Josie. Motioning to her coach for a substitute, she stepped to the side of the court. "I need a breather," she said to him.

He pulled her off to the side and sent in an underclassman to replace her position. "Are you okay?"

How many times would she be asked that exact question? She was far from okay, but wanted to assess how bad the damage was in private, without all these eyes on her—eyes that would no doubt lead to her having to sit out a game, or worse, the season. She grimaced. "It hurts," she admitted.

"What hurts?" Coach Jackson leveled his gaze with her. "Shelly," he said, calling to the assistant coach. "Take over for a minute."

Logan shook her head. "I'm fine. I just need a minute." Normally, Coach Newcomb, or Shelly, as he called her, would have tended to an injured player, and Coach Jackson would have stayed at the bench. But this was apparently no ordinary situation. Behind them, she heard Coach Newcomb call a time-out.

This was ridiculous. There was no need to burn a time-out so early in a tight game. She wanted to tell the coach as much, but the intensity of the pain brought her back to her problems for the moment.

"It's my shoulder," she said, deciding the quicker they got to the bottom of this, the quicker she could go back in the game.

She closed her eyes, wishing the Tylenol she'd taken would have done its job, although to be fair, its job wasn't to prevent further injury. She opened her eyes, looking down at her shoulder. It looked normal, other than a little swollen, but any slight movement proved normal was a lie.

Across from her, Coach Jackson had called over the team trainer to take a look.

"Can you lift it in a lateral motion?" she asked.

"Yeah," Logan said confidently. She attempted the move the trainer was making, and bit her lip to stifle her cry of pain.

"So that's a no," the trainer said, shaking her head. "If you can't do it without pain, don't. Can you rotate it?"

Logan shook her head. She'd already tried once, and as much as she wanted back on that court, she was sure the pain might make her pass out.

The trainer reached up, gently feeling around her shoulder. "She needs to see a doctor," she said after a moment to the coach. "You need an MRI," she said, turning her attention to Logan.

Logan opened her mouth to protest, but the trainer was already talking to Coach Jackson. "You can go back to the game. I'll make sure she's taken care of. She's not going back in tonight."

"Logan, what do you need?"

His question was so broad. What did she need? A new shoulder, a drink of water, some pain pills, and to get back in the game. Behind them, the game was already back in motion.

"What do you think it is?" she asked, ignoring the question.

"I'd need to see the MRI," the trainer said, shoving her hands in her pocket, "but just on the spot, I'd say a rotator cuff tear."

"No," Logan said, shaking her head. "It can't be that."

Coach Jackson put a hand on her good shoulder. "Logan, you need to take care of that. It's not going to heal on its own. Let's hope for the best, and err on the side of caution. Go ahead and get to a doctor tonight. We'll win this one for you." He glanced back at the court, then back to Logan. "In the meantime, I can't have my all-star shooting guard sitting out here in excruciating pain." He offered her the best winning smile he could muster. "There's still a lot of season left."

The words were meant to be reassuring, she knew. She nodded and gave a half-hearted smile. There was a lot of season left, but that also meant a lot for her to miss out on, if it was a serious injury.

As the trainer led her down to the locker room, she gave in to the tears that filled her eyes.

"I'm so sorry, Logan," she said, patting her on the back gently. "I know it's hard news to take in, but we don't know anything for sure yet." She led the way to the medical room. "Let's get some ice on it, and then I'm going to have someone drive you to the hospital. Are your parents here?"

The tears came harder, as she shook her head. Her mom was back in Arizona, and her dad had another late case. Ben had an away game, so she had no family in the stands. She straightened her shoulders and reached up to dry her tears. She had Carter. "I have someone who can take me," she said after a moment. "Just let me text her."

Before she could open up her text messaging app, Carter had already texted her. She opened the message.

Are you okay? Where'd they take you? I left my stuff with Aiden, and I'll come meet you at the hospital or take you home.

She scrunched up her face, warding off another onslaught of tears and clenched her jaw.

I need a ride to the hospital, she typed back. *Meet me at the back of the gym, please.*

The last thing she wanted to do was walk through a sea of well-meaning fans who'd no doubt make her voice her greatest fears, that it was a season-ending injury. Instead, she'd rather slink out the back and collapse into Carter's arms, where she could fall apart if she needed to. A fresh wave of pain shot through her body as she maneuvered herself onto the bench seat.

The trainer fastened an ice pack over Logan's shoulder and wrapped tape over it to keep it in place. "That should hold until they get you in to see the doctor," she said. The look of pity on her face made Logan want to cry even more. Whenever people gave you that look, it was never good news.

"Thank you," she said, nodding as she stood. "Hope the rest of the night is uneventful for you."

"Me too. Straight to the hospital." Her tone was stern but kind.

Logan nodded. In the locker room, she gathered her things and hoisted her bag onto her good shoulder. She went to remove her jersey, but couldn't get out of it on her own. Kicking the floor in protest, she untucked the top and headed for the back door.

"What happened?" Carter asked, taking her bag as she opened the door.

"It's my shoulder." Logan pointed to the huge ice pack pushing her neck to the side.

"Are you okay?" Her face had gone ashen, as she looked Logan up and down.

She must look as bad as she felt. She nodded, then shook her head, then shrugged her one good shoulder. "It hurts," she said. "A lot. I've had pain in it since the accident, but it's been bearable. I think I injured it then and didn't give it time to heal. Now, it's gotten worse."

"Hop in," Carter said, motioning to her car that she'd pulled up to the door. "I'll get you over to the hospital. Do you want me to call your dad or Ben?"

"Not yet." Logan shook her head. Would they even see her without a parent? "My dad is still at the office. Ben is at a game."

"I'll call your mom," Carter said decisively. "But first, I'll get you to the hospital. Presbyterian or UNM?" she asked.

"Whichever is closest," Logan said, shaking her head. The only time she'd been to an emergency room in recent history, she'd been so out of it, she had no idea which one it had been. "Thank you."

Carter grabbed her hand, holding it tightly while she drove, and even though Logan wanted to cry, she couldn't help but feel safe.

CHAPTER NINETEEN

In true New Mexico fashion, the sun shone down, brighter and warmer than it had any reason for in late January, but Carter was thankful for a break from the cold. She removed her jacket, casting it over her arm, soaking up the sun before heading into the grocery store. Once inside, she walked through the aisles and tried to think of comforting items.

What was an appropriate consolation prize for having to spend the next three and a half weeks in a sling, followed by missing the rest of your senior year in the sport you loved? Carter shook her head. It wasn't her responsibility to fix the problem, and she knew she couldn't, even if it was. Still, there had to be something she could do.

Once the pain meds had worn off and Logan's dad had arrived, surgery had been scheduled, and it had been a whirlwind of events. Carter thought back to the past week of waiting for Logan to text first, so she didn't disturb her if the pain meds had given her some much needed rest. She missed her sweet and happy Logan. She just missed her in general.

With her dad back at work, her mom back in Arizona, and Ben at an out-of-town game, Carter had volunteered to be her nurse for the day. It was a task she was happy to fulfill, if anything, just to see Logan and to make sure she was okay. But now as she perused the store, she didn't know what to bring.

Logan had insisted she didn't need anything special, but Carter knew she'd have brought her something special even if it was just a regular day. She stopped in front of the flower section, smiling back at the memory of the rose Logan had brought her on their first date. Picking out a small bouquet, she placed it gingerly into the cart.

After securing a few snack items, she headed for the checkout. *I'm on my way*, she texted Logan so she didn't surprise her.

When she pulled into the driveway, she looked up at the large house. She'd been here several times, but never inside. Her smile grew as she saw Logan standing out front, waving at her with her good arm.

"I'd offer to help carry stuff in, but I'm not much help in that area these days," Logan said, offering a sad smile and motioning to her sling.

"I've got it," Carter said, grabbing the bag and the flowers. "These," she said, extending the bouquet as she approached, "are for you."

Logan accepted the gift, smiling as she sniffed the petals. "You really are the best." She leaned against the door to keep it open. "Come in."

"Where are you laid up for the day?" Carter asked, looking around.

"Up here." Logan nodded to the stairs. "I've tried the living room, but it's just not as comfy as my bed."

"Let's get you back in bed then," Carter said, following Logan's lead.

"I really thought the first time you said that to me, it would feel a little less like medical advice." Logan laughed.

That laughter was a sound Carter hadn't heard since before the game. She smiled, savoring its melody. "Next time I say it, it'll have a different meaning," Carter promised.

"Good," Logan said, pulling the door closed behind them. "Welcome to my room."

Carter looked around the walls, noting that Logan had placed her framed photo across from her bed, where she could look at it whenever she wanted. "I like it." She motioned to the bed. "Go ahead and lay down. I'm going to go heat this soup up, put those flowers in a vase, and I'll be back up." She glanced at the TV. "We can watch a movie or something."

"But first," Logan said, kissing her, "I get to greet my gorgeous girlfriend. This week really has been the worst, and just seeing you put me in the best mood."

"I'm happy to be here," Carter said, kissing her once more, and helping her to the bed. "I'll be right back."

Taking extra care to keep the flowers fresh, Carter trimmed the stems. She didn't want to dig through all of the Watts's things, so she opted for a mason jar from the glass cabinet and put them in water. After heating the soup her mom had made, she carried both items back up the stairs.

"Here you are," she said, sliding the flowers onto the bedside table, and handing the soup over to Logan, who sat propped up on pillows. "The soup is from my mom. She hopes you feel better. I reminded her it was your shoulder, but she insisted on making soup. She said that pain meds can lead to upset stomachs, so soup was the best option. I tried to score you some of her empanadas, but she said she'd make them for you when you're all healed up."

"That's very sweet of her. Please tell her I am very grateful."

"I will," Carter said, taking a seat on the opposite side of the bed. "She likes you, by the way."

"Even though the second time she met me, I had you pinned up against a wall, kissing you like I'd never kissed you before?"

Carter laughed. "Even after that, she thinks you're pretty amazing."

Logan took a sip of the soup and smiled. "She's forgiving and a hell of a cook."

With a nod, Carter ripped into the extra bag of gummy bears she'd bought. "One for you. One for me," Carter said, scooting the other bag up toward Logan's hand.

She looked up to find Logan watching her with a grin. "What is it?"

"One kiss is never enough," Logan said, leaning closer.

Right before their lips met, Logan pulled back.

"Dammit," she said, looking down at the puddle of soup on her shirt and sweatpants.

"It's okay," Carter said with a laugh. "We'll get you cleaned up, and then I'll come to you for a kiss." She stood, collecting what was left of the soup and placing the bowl on the bedside table.

"I'll get a towel. What else do you need?"

"I'm going to need help to…" Logan looked down at the floor and frowned. "I can't get in and out of a shirt by myself."

"I'm here to help," Carter said, placing a kiss on top of Logan's head. Her heart raced as she headed down the stairs to grab a towel. When she returned, Logan had gathered a fresh T-shirt and laid it on the edge of the bed. She'd already changed out of her sweatpants, and for that, Carter was grateful. She might not have been a real nurse, but she was pretty sure some of the rules about not being in a compromising situation with your patient still applied, even if the patient was your girlfriend.

Logan accepted the towel and cleaned up the mess, before turning to Carter. "You know, I always thought the first time you got me out of my clothes would be different too." She raised an eyebrow and pointed to her soiled shirt.

Carter walked over, keeping eye contact as she gently pulled the shirt over Logan's head. She wasn't prepared for Logan to put her good arm around her waist and pull her closer. Her heart pounded, and every sense tingled, as Logan held her there, pressed up against her bare flesh.

"Just wanted to make sure it wasn't a complete waste, you getting me out of my clothes," Logan said, kissing her slowly. As she backed away, she held up her good arm for her shirt. Carter held out the simple black T-shirt, wishing she could savor the moment without Logan being in pain.

Biting her lip, she moved into motion, securing the shirt around Logan's body. As Logan climbed back into bed, Carter reached for the remote. She needed a distraction to keep her sane. Somehow, Logan Watts was sensual and in control, even after surgery had left her in a sling.

"What would you like to watch?" she asked, still trying to catch her breath.

Beside her, Logan laughed. "You're going to have to turn that around," she said, pointing to the remote.

Carter looked down, realizing she was mashing the power button, while pointing the wrong end at the TV screen.

"Right," Carter said, nodding and fumbling the remote as she flipped it around.

"It's okay to be a little flustered," Logan said, biting her lip. "In fact, I kind of like it."

"Yeah?"

"Yeah. It means you still think I'm attractive, even when I look like a mess." Logan gestured to her T-shirt and sweats.

"You could never be a mess."

Logan shook her head and laughed. "Regardless, I don't care what we watch." She looked up to the ceiling and brought her finger to her chin. "What would you be watching if you were at home?"

Powering the TV on, Carter propped herself up on a pillow. She turned her attention to Logan, eyeing her carefully. "I'm debating if it's too soon to show my nerdy side."

"Show me all the sides," Logan said, smiling as she nodded to the TV.

"Have you had any time to immerse yourself into the world of queer ladies on-screen?"

Logan raised an eyebrow and shook her head, her dimple showing as she grinned. "Enlighten me. You're pretty good at that already."

"We've got a handful of shows we could pick from, depending on what you're in the mood for," Carter said. Mentally, she ran through a list of her favorites. "If you want to see the nerdy side, where I'll get engrossed in something a little on the sci-fi side of things, I vote *Wynonna Earp* or *Arcane*. If you want something funny, *One Day at a Time*. If you're into superheroes, we'll go with *Batwoman*."

"Any of those sound amazing, as long as you'll come up here and snuggle with me while we watch," Logan said, smiling sweetly and patting the pillow next to her.

Moving up the bed, Carter put an arm around Logan and situated the pillows so she could comfortably sit up while watching the show. Flipping over to Netflix, she queued up *Wynonna Earp*. Before she hit play, she looked over at Logan. "We're going to watch this one, because for next Halloween, I want to go with you as…" She paused. "I don't want to ruin it, but there are two characters on here that'll make sense when you see them. That is, assuming you haven't kicked me to the curb by October."

She knew she was playing a risky game. They hadn't talked a long-term future, but everything just made so much sense, it seemed like they might as well at least start the conversation, and it gave her a perfect segue into her big news.

"Halloween, huh?" Logan turned to face Carter. "I'm not planning on kicking you anywhere, but…" She looked at the TV and then back to Carter. "Aren't you going to be in New York by then?"

Carter smiled, shaking her head. "I was waiting for the right time to tell you, when things weren't so crazy. I'm sticking around. I'll be a University of New Mexico Lobo right along with you."

"You didn't do this because of me, did you?" Logan asked, her brow furrowing. "I'd never want to stand in the way of your dreams."

"It's not about you," Carter said, placing a kiss on the top of Logan's head. It wasn't, and Carter had made sure to make this choice with no outside factors involved.

"What made you pick UNM?"

"The Journalism program is really hard to beat," Carter said, smiling as she finally told Logan the news she'd been debating for months. "Carolyn brought in a guest speaker to talk with me the other day. He's a local journalist, who studied at UNM. He talked about the program, the hands-on experience, the opportunities, and it just clicked. For me, New York had always been this big-city dream, where I hoped I could start a new life, dive into gay culture, and really just launch some sort of magical journey that had so many firsts. I think I wanted to have that starving artist period for the glamor of it all, not the harsh reality of the situation. But that's all it was, some sort of daydream that I'd be a new me." She looked at Logan and shook her head. "I don't want to be a new me. I want to flourish here, where I'll actually still get a taste of my home culture, I'll be close enough to see my mom from time to time, I'll have the chance to build the gay culture here, and I'll have so many more opportunities."

"Are you sure?" Logan had yet to smile at the news, and Carter took a deep breath.

"I'm sure. I debated for months, and I'm not ready to leave here. I'll visit New York one of these days, and when the time is right, I may move there. Or somewhere else." She looked up to the ceiling and then back to Logan. "I may only stick around UNM a couple of years. But student loans don't come without a steep price tag. Everything here is paid for, and while I'd invest a million dollars of debt into my dreams, I don't think it's actually worth it if I can't commit to pulling the trigger." She pulled Logan in closer. "I'm not giving up on my dreams. I'm chasing them, where it feels right. And, I'm not settling for UNM," she added. "Trust me, I've debated that a million times too. I did a lot of soul-searching on my intentions before coming to this decision, and while it looks like the safer call, I think it's actually the bolder move for me. It forces me to grow and to challenge myself to adapt to a brand new world—right here. I think I'll like that much more."

"In that case, I'm really happy to hear that." Logan wrapped her fingers around Carter's hand and smiled.

"As a bonus, I'll get to watch you back on the court." She kissed Logan slowly. "No pressure on anything though. If you get to college and decide you want to fly solo, we'll roll with those punches too."

"I appreciate the sentiment," Logan said, smiling slowly. "But can you please stop talking about breaking up for a minute?" She laughed. "If we have to cross that bridge, we will. For now though, I'd love nothing more than to cuddle with you and watch your show, with the promise of couples costumes for Halloween."

"You've got it," Carter agreed, hitting the play button and pulling Logan in closer.

In the middle of the second episode, Logan sat straight up in bed. "Oh my god, it *is* going to be gay!" She smiled at Carter, watching as Officer Nicole Haught flirted with Waverly Earp onscreen. "Is that who you want to be for Halloween?"

"I think you'd make a good-looking officer for a night," Carter said, biting her lip. She closed her eyes, imagining the sight. "We'll dress up, go out on the town or maybe to some kind of college party, and just have the best time."

"Sign me up for that," Logan said, nodding. "All of that. In fact, I'm pretty sure I'd dress as one of those demons on the show if it would make you bite your lip like that."

As the show played in the background, Carter's heart raced. Logan ran her fingers up and down Carter's arm, setting her skin on fire with each touch. Throwing caution to the wind, she rolled over, positioning herself above Logan. Just a few kisses couldn't hurt.

Logan's eyes shone with desire, as Carter closed the distance between their lips. Savoring each taste, each feeling of Logan's lips against hers, she sighed. She gently bit Logan's bottom lip, and remembering the soft sigh that had escaped the night of the picnic, she moved lower, kissing the soft skin of Logan's neck.

"Wait," Logan said, breathlessly.

Carter pulled back, sitting up quickly. "I'm sorry. I didn't mean to cross a line."

"No, it's not that." Logan shook her head. Running her hands through her hair, she brushed it out of her face. "I just wanted to tell you you're not the only one who's been doing a lot of thinking." She gestured around the room. "I've been pretty much confined in here, so I've had a lot of time to think about things."

"What kind of things?"

"You and me," Logan said. "I'm ready."

The words sent a shiver of anticipation through Carter's body. "Aren't you on pain medications and stuff?" She looked down at the floor. As much as she wanted to do this with Logan, she wasn't going to let their first experience take place on questionable ground.

"Nope," Logan shook her head. "Not today. I have been for most of the week, but I wanted to be clear-headed today to see you." She ran a finger up Carter's arm. "You know, just in case you were ready too."

Carter nodded. She appreciated a planner. "If you're sure," she said, climbing back over Logan's body.

"I'm one hundred percent sure," Logan said, her voice deep with desire. "I'll tell you if I'm not."

Her heart racing, Carter looked down, taking in every detail of Logan's face. Her lips slightly parted, as she smiled, waiting and ready. Carter kissed her long and slow, sliding her hands over Logan's waist. At her touch, Logan leaned her head back, nodding.

"I'm going to need help getting out of this," she said, pointing down to her shirt. "Can you give me a hand?"

Carter nodded, sitting back and grabbing the hem of Logan's shirt. Carefully pulling it over Logan's head, she marveled at the sight before her. As she reached up to explore the exposed skin, she figured if she were religious, this would be her idea of heaven.

A knock on the door caused her to jump from the bed.

"Oh my god," Logan whispered, reaching for her shirt. "Who is it?" she called out, breathless.

Carter's mind raced. She'd watched Logan lock the door.

"Are you okay in there, Logan?" a man's voice called out, which Carter had to assume had come from Logan's dad.

Her mouth fell open, as she looked around the room. Should she find a hiding spot? Jump out the window, maybe?

"Yeah, just give me a second," Logan said, handing Carter her shirt and motioning for her to put it on. Slipping her into the garment, Carter held up her hands in question.

"Sit down," Logan mouthed, pointing to the opposite side of the bed. Carter nodded and quietly took a seat. Grabbing the remote, she turned her attention to the screen as Logan opened the door.

"Hey," her dad said, wrapping Logan into a hug. "How are you feeling?"

"I'm fine," Logan said, her voice much higher than normal. Carter's heart pounded as she looked up and offered a wave. "My friend Carter came over to take care of me. We were just watching a show on TV. You're home early." Her words were tumbling out at rapid speed, and Carter silently urged her to slow down.

"Hi, Carter," he said, returning the wave. "Have you been sleeping?" He asked, turning his attention back to Logan and pointing to her tousled hair.

"Yeah," she lied. "I've been resting off and on. Carter just got here a little while ago to keep me company."

"Well, I won't keep you," he said, smiling at his daughter. "I'll just be downstairs if you two need anything." He turned to Carter. "Thanks for coming by to check on her. That's the sign of a good friend."

With that, he turned and headed down the stairs. Logan closed the door behind him, and slid down into the floor. She buried her head in her hands. "We need to find a solution to that problem soon," she whispered. "First your mom, then almost my dad." She stood, and Carter walked over to her.

Taking Logan's beet-red face into her hands, she nodded. "We'll figure something out. In the meantime, should I go? Do you want me to stay?"

"I want so many things," Logan said, laughing. She shook her head. "I don't want you to go, but maybe you should sit over on that side, just in case he comes back."

Carter nodded, sliding back to the opposite side of the bed. She tried to focus on the show and still her breathing, but the memory of Logan's body sprawled out beneath her offered a much better form of entertainment.

CHAPTER TWENTY

A candle flickered in the corner of her room, wafting the scent of lavender throughout the air. A gift from Carter, it was meant to help her relax. Logan flipped through the pages of the book she'd ordered online about recovery after trauma. It was geared more toward a parent talking to their teenager about difficult experiences, but she'd been learning from it just the same.

Trauma. The word played on a loop in her head. She'd seen her share of it, first with Luke, then with her injury, not that the two could be compared. But both flipped her world upside down, forcing her into unknown territory.

Closing the book, she laid it on the bedside table. She stretched her neck and smiled, proud of all that she'd managed to accomplish over the past several weeks, even with an injury. Mindfulness and meditation had become her saving graces. Coupled with her visits from Carter, her classes, and getting to travel with the team, even though she couldn't suit out, she'd found ways to cope with the loss of the season.

As she rose for the day, she lifted her shoulder, slowly practicing her physical therapy. Thankful to have the sling gone, she took a shower and got dressed with renewed excitement. Today wasn't only a new beginning for her, but it was also her first day back to the grind. She'd been attending classes and games, but for the most part had stayed holed up in her room, intent on healing completely so she didn't have to miss out on anything in the future. She looked at the calendar on her wall, seeing today's date with a huge smiley face written under it. Carter had scrawled it on there, her first day of freedom. She closed her eyes, momentarily dreaming about the possibilities of going on dates and getting back in the groove of regular life.

She checked her phone and smiled. Just a little longer, and her mother would be home—this time for good. It felt like she'd missed so much, and Logan couldn't wait to hug her and tell her about everything.

She paused halfway down the staircase and took a deep breath. *Everything?* Was she ready for that? Was her mom? She chewed on the inside of her cheek, bringing her hands together and considering the possibilities. She'd always gone to her mom with everything. But with her having been gone for so long, Logan had gone through some of the biggest changes in her life. She clenched her jaw.

Before she could decide anything, the front door swung wide open with her mom and grandma behind it.

"We're home!" her mom called out, heaving a suitcase into the entryway.

"Mom!" Logan exclaimed, forgoing her fears and running to greet her mother. She pulled her into a hug and held her close for almost a full minute. "I'm so glad you're home." She turned her attention to her grandma and gave her a warm hug. "I'm so glad you're here too. Welcome home!"

She ushered them inside, grabbing the suitcase with her good arm and walking it back to her parents' bedroom. In a matter of seconds, Ben and her dad came rushing into the room, and the house was full of hugs, laughter, and questions about the trip.

They got their grandma situated in the guest bedroom, and Logan turned to Ben. "Want to come with me to grab some pizza to celebrate?" she asked, glancing at her phone. "It's almost lunchtime, and that way no one has to cook."

"I'm still getting used to the idea of you chauffeuring me around these days," he said, laughing and tossing her the keys from his pocket. "I'll ride with you."

After a quick trip down the street, they returned with two large pizzas in tow. Over lunch, conversation flowed easily, ranging from Logan's recovery to her grandma's to Ben's debut on the varsity basketball team. When their grandma returned to her room for an afternoon nap, Ben headed out to see his friends, and her dad went back to the office, Logan's breath caught in her throat. She dropped the stack of paper plates she was holding from clearing the table. Grabbing them once more, she tried to steady her breathing. It was as if the air had gone from the room, even though she knew she didn't *have* to tell her mom.

"What's wrong, honey?" Her mom came up beside her, steadying her as she stood. "Are you in pain?"

"No, I'm fine." Logan tried to manage a smile but failed. "It's not my shoulder. I'm okay."

"What is it?" Her mom took the plates from her hand and carried them into the kitchen. Tossing them in the trash can, she turned to face Logan who still stood in the kitchen.

She opened her mouth, but the words wouldn't come. She shook her head, shoving her hands in her pockets.

"You look like you've seen a ghost." The concern in her mom's voice was almost enough to break her. Setting her jaw, she took a deep breath.

"I think I want to talk to you about something," she said slowly, carefully choosing each word. "But I think it might be hard to talk about."

Across from her, her mother straightened her shoulders and nodded. Logan knew from years of observing that it was her best game face. Inside, her mother might be as nervous as could be, but she'd put on a brave face in order to make life easier on her kids. Logan gulped. She didn't want to rock the boat, not on her first day back, but her heart pounded, nagging her to continue.

"You can tell me anything," her mom said, motioning to the barstools at the counter. "Let's have a seat."

Logan nodded, sitting beside her. It had always been true in the past, but would this change things? She gripped the edge of the counter so hard her knuckles were turning white. Putting her hands in her lap, she took a deep breath.

Next to her, her mom sat patiently, placing a hand on her good shoulder and offering unspoken support.

"This is kind of hard," Logan admitted after a moment. She felt tears sting the corners of her eyes, but blinked them away.

"I've been resisting the urge to ask," her mom said gently, "but there are a million things running through my mind. Are you okay? Are you pregnant, in trouble, or something else?"

Logan laughed, thankful for a moment of levity. She was definitely *not* pregnant.

"No," she said, shaking her head, dismissing the worries. "It's nothing like that. I'm not even having sex." As soon as the words escaped her mouth, she leaned back. One of these days she was going to learn to use a filter. While that was true for now, she didn't know how much longer it would be. She smiled nervously, while her mom nodded.

"So that's not what this is about?"

Logan shook her head. In a way it was, but it was about so much more. "I'm seeing someone," she said after a moment.

Her mom smiled. "Good. I'm glad to hear it. I know you weren't too upset by the breakup with Barrett, but I'm happy to hear you're out there exploring other options."

What an interesting choice of words. Logan looked down to the floor, working to practice the mindfulness tactics she'd learned. The unpleasant feelings of doubt and worry were normal, and it was okay to feel them, even if she hated them.

"Why are you so nervous?" Her mom's words broke her thought process. "We've always talked openly about things. Tell me about him."

Logan cleared her throat. It was now or never. She now had to either lie on the spot, or come clean. Gripping the base of the barstool for support, she nodded. "I can't tell you about a him, but I can tell you about her." She paused, waiting for any negative reaction.

Her mom tilted her head to the side and raised an eyebrow. For a moment, she didn't speak. "Go on," she said finally.

"Her name is Carter." She looked down at the floor and closed her eyes. "She's the smartest, funniest person I've ever met, and when we started hanging out, I realized that I didn't just want to be her friend."

"I'd like to meet her." Her mom's words were matter-of-fact, but she smiled. "I'm glad you told me. I can imagine that was a hard thing to do."

"You're not mad or upset?"

Her mom shook her head. "I'm processing it, but I've always trusted your judgment. Even as a kid, you had a pretty good head on your shoulders. If you think she's right for you, I'll be in your corner supporting you every step of the way."

"Do you think dad's going to take it okay?"

"He'll be just fine, and if he isn't right away, he'll adjust." She reached out, pulling Logan into a hug. "We had a discussion when you three were just babies, and we knew that, whatever and whoever you grew up to be, we were going to love you just the same as we did in those early days. Nothing," she said, bringing her hand up under Logan's chin to make sure Logan heard and understood, "will stand in the way of that."

The tears she'd held at bay now spilled onto her cheeks. "I love you."

"I love you too." Her mother held her close. "How long have you been together?" she asked, pulling back.

"Since before Christmas," Logan said. She smiled nervously.

"Then it's about time I meet her."

"You will," Logan promised. She glanced at her phone. "I'm actually going over to see her this afternoon. I'm going to ask her to the spring formal, so maybe you'll get to meet her when she comes to pick me up."

"Show me a picture." Her mom gestured to her phone.

"Okay." Logan grabbed her phone. Her hands were shaking from the range of emotions, but she scrolled through to find the selfie they'd taken at the top of the Tram. She smiled at the memory, showing the photo to her mom. "Before you ask, those are virgin mojitos," she said, laughing as she watched her mom nod.

"She's really pretty," she said, taking the phone for a closer look. "Even more than that, you two look really happy, and that's what matters."

"You're the best," Logan said, hugging her once more. "I'm really thankful you're home."

"It's good to be home. No more missing out on things." Her mom stretched and yawned. "I'm probably going to go take a nap. That drive was rough." She glanced at the clock on the wall. "Are you headed out for your date?"

"In just a bit," Logan said, smiling as she stood in front of her mother, for the first time in months feeling as though she had nothing to hide.

"Have fun and be safe," she said, standing and heading for the doorway. She turned back and smiled. "Don't forget to tell her I want to meet her, and don't be out late."

"You've got it."

As she left the room, Logan leaned up against the countertop. Texting Carter, she decided she could head over there a little early. It had been weeks since they'd had the chance to hang out and be truly alone. Gathering her things, she headed for the door. On the drive over, she stopped to pick up a handful of flowers from the store.

She checked her reflection in the rearview mirror and smiled. Even though she was ninety-nine percent sure Carter would agree to go to the dance, her heart fluttered. As she pulled up, she saw Annie's car in the driveway and cringed. She was a really nice lady, but Logan was sure she'd never be able to face her without remembering how she'd caught Logan and Carter. Logan took a deep breath, gripping the steering wheel.

"Now or never," she whispered to herself. There had been a lot of that for one day.

Straightening her shirt, she stood and walked up to the front door. She thought about texting, but opted to knock instead. If she was going to be bold, she was going to do it right.

"Logan," Annie said, opening the door with a smile on her face. "I figured it must be you, since Carter yelled out from the top of the stairs that she'd get the door." Annie ushered her in, the clear delight at making Logan squirm evident on her face. She might have liked Logan, but she also clearly enjoyed getting a bit of humor out of the situation. "You brought flowers," she said, keeping her voice low. Her face lit up into the biggest smile she'd ever cast Logan's direction. "You are a keeper. Go on up. She's in her room."

"Thanks," Logan said, making her way past Annie and climbing the stairs toward Carter's room.

"I'm coming," Carter called out, opening the door right as Logan reached it. "Oh, hey," she said, smiling first at Logan and then at the flowers. "Come in," she added, moving out of the doorway.

"I've missed you," Logan said as the door closed behind her.

"You saw me yesterday." Carter smiled as she accepted the flowers. "Thank you for these by the way."

"You're very welcome," Logan said, performing a mock curtsy. She cringed inwardly. They'd been dating for almost three months. She had no idea why she was still so awkward at times. "Also, just because I saw you yesterday doesn't mean I didn't miss you." She laughed nervously. "But I miss getting to hang out with you and spend time away from my room."

"Your room isn't so bad all the time." Carter pulled her in for a kiss. "I seem to remember some good moments in there."

Logan nodded. "There were some good times, huh? A handful of stolen kisses, lots of TV binges, and times when you held me so close, it felt like you were holding me together."

"Yeah, that was pretty nice." Carter looked at Logan and then to her bed. She raised an eyebrow.

"Absolutely not," Logan said, laughing. "Not with your mom here. I'm not going to risk that. While we're here, I'm the model citizen dating her daughter."

"Reform looks good on you," Carter said, placing her finger under Logan's chin and kissing her again softly. "Since we're here for the afternoon, what did you have in mind?"

"I actually wanted to talk," Logan said, shoving her hands in her pocket. She took a deep breath, and Carter frowned.

"Oh no." Carter took a step backward. "Okay." She took a seat on the bed and placed her hands on her knees, as if bracing herself.

"No." Logan held up her hands. "Nothing bad. I wanted to ask you to do something for me, with me?"

"To you?" Carter teased, rebounding from her negative response quickly.

"Well, yes, but first." She smiled confidently. "Will you be my date to the spring formal?"

"Does that mean matching outfits, going together, and people knowing we're there together?"

Logan nodded, her smile growing as Carter considered the thought.

"Are you ready?"

"I am," she said, grabbing Carter's hands. "I'm not planning a grand announcement. I'm just going to show up with you on my arm and not give a damn what anyone says. You're the most amazing person, and I can't wait to show you off."

"God, I love you," Carter said. Just as quickly, she shook her head. "I mean…well…I mean it, but I…" She looked down to the ground. "I wasn't going to say it like that."

Logan laughed, pulling Carter to her. "I love you too," she said, holding her close. She leaned back and raised an eyebrow. "Is that yes to the dance, though?"

With a laugh, Carter stood and spun Logan around the floor. "It's a definite yes."

"Good," Logan said, sitting on the edge of Carter's bed and motioning for Carter to join her. "That means we have outfits to plan."

CHAPTER TWENTY-ONE

With one final look in the mirror, Carter admired her outfit. She would have loved the sleek black suit and skinny gold tie regardless, but paired with Logan's black and gold dress, it was going to be perfect. She added her gold stud earrings and a spritz of perfume.

"You look stunning," her mom called out from the bottom of the stairs when she made her entrance. Carter had to laugh, wondering how long she'd been standing there, just waiting for Carter to emerge. "I still wish Logan was coming by here to take pictures."

"Her mom insisted," Carter said with a shrug.

"I know," her mom said, waving her hand through the air. "It's fine. She deserves that moment too. I want copies though."

"You'll get them," Carter assured her, kissing her on the cheek. "I'll see you tomorrow."

"Where do Logan's parents think she's spending the night?" her mom asked, a knowing look on her face.

"They know she's staying at Josie's. We both are," Carter said. She wasn't going to sugarcoat the truth. Her mom deserved more than that.

"Okay, as long as you're safe."

Carter nodded. "Promise," she said, grabbing her keys and heading for the door.

"Text if you need anything. Offer still stands."

"I know. Thank you," Carter said, closing the door behind her.

On the drive, she turned up the sound, letting the sweet music of the playlist Logan had created for her and shared with her drown out any of her nerves. Carter had been out for two years, but this was all new territory for Logan. As she pulled into the driveway, she counted the cars. The entire family was home. She took a deep breath and looked at her reflection in the rearview mirror. They all knew, and Logan had said they were fine with it. She just hoped they were ready for a girl in a suit. Standing outside the car, she adjusted her jacket and grabbed the corsage she'd bought for Logan.

For once, she was grateful their pretentious private school held an inordinate amount of dances. Closing her eyes briefly, she remembered the way Logan had looked at the last one. With renewed enthusiasm, she headed for the steps. She raised her hand to knock on the door, but it swung open in front of her.

"Come in." Logan's mom was smiling from ear to ear. She looked Carter up and down. "You look absolutely beautiful." She extended a hand. "I'm Stephanie. You must be Carter."

"It's wonderful to meet you," Carter said, shaking her hand as she stepped inside.

"So good to finally meet you too. I've made Logan tell me everything about you. She's in here, by the way." Stephanie motioned down the hallway. "Putting on some final touches." She turned to Logan's dad, who was standing in the living room. "Jeff," she said to him, "this is Carter."

"We've met a time or two," he said. "It's good to see you again, Carter." He smiled at her, but Carter could see the knowing look in his eyes, no doubt replaying all the times she'd been in Logan's room with the door closed. She offered him a smile, trying her best to keep her heart from pounding out of her chest under his stare.

Fortunately, Logan walked into the living room, and he turned his attention to her. Melting like a teddy bear, he smiled broadly and walked across the room. "You are beautiful," he said, taking her in his arms.

Carter stared. Beautiful didn't even scratch the surface. With her long hair flowing down her back, pinned up on the sides, and her long, halter-top black dress with golden accents, she was a work of art. Logan turned to Carter. The blue in her eyes seemed to pop even more than usual, and Carter thought she might melt under the intensity of Logan's stare.

"You…" Logan said, wide-eyed. "You look amazing."

"Same goes for you," Carter said. She wanted to say so much more, but she bit her tongue. There would be time for more intimate compliments later. As they posed for pictures, she couldn't help but feel that this was how it was always supposed to be. No one was making a big deal about the same-sex couple or going out of their way to act differently. They simply were a couple, and that was that. She was relieved to have it out in the open, proudly taking her place by Logan's side. By the time they got to the car, Logan reached for Carter's hand.

"You look incredible," she said, once they were alone. " I absolutely love that suit. It's so hot. I didn't have the words to tell you in there."

"I was thinking the same thing," Carter said with a laugh. "I wanted to be respectful in front of your parents, but damn!" She glanced toward the window of the house, where her dad and mom were watching them. "Let's go," she said, nodding in their direction with a laugh.

"Yes, take me somewhere without an audience."

"Where we're going, there's a much bigger audience than that," Carter said, pointing behind her shoulder. "Are you ready for it?"

"More than ever," Logan said, grabbing her hand. "You're listening to the playlist?" She smiled, humming along to Dua Lipa's "If It Ain't Me."

"It's my favorite," Carter said. She looked at Logan. "You're my favorite, actually. Seeing as how you made it and you have really good taste in music, it automatically wins."

Beside her, Logan met her gaze. She pressed her lips together and shook her head with a smile. "You really are the most amazing person I've ever met."

"The feeling's mutual," Carter said, as she pulled into the school parking lot.

Walking around to Logan's side of the car, she reached out her arm, beaming with pride as Logan looped her arm through Carter's. As they walked through the entryway of the gymnasium, Carter could hear a couple of gasps. She heard Logan's name on a whisper, and gripped Logan's hand to offer support.

Undeterred, Logan smiled proudly, straightening her shoulders, as they stepped up to the photographer to have their photograph taken. The taller of the two, Logan stood behind Carter, wrapping her arms around Carter's waist and smiling for the camera.

As they made their way to a table, Carter looked at her, an eyebrow raised in question.

"Just happy to be here," Logan said. With a playful grin, she grabbed Carter's hand and pulled her to the dance floor, not wasting a single second. As the music thumped, Carter couldn't take her eyes off Logan. Rhythm, beauty, brains, and not a care in the world.

"You two look amazing," Josie said, coming up beside them. She placed her hands on her face and looked from Logan to Carter and back again. "It's all anyone's talking about."

"Are you sure that's the part they're talking about?" Logan asked with a laugh.

"No one has anything bad to say from what I've heard, and I'll make sure they don't. I think they're impressed, more than anything." Josie looked them both up and down with a nod of approval. "Besides, who cares what they think? You two were clearly made for each other."

"I'd have to agree," Logan said, pulling Carter close and kissing her boldly for the world to see.

As they danced and laughed throughout the night, Carter couldn't help but think that it was just as the cliché banner hanging over the stage suggested: *a night to remember*. By the time they arrived at Josie's for the after-party, Carter was sure she didn't want any of the drinks that were available. The high she was on from being in Logan's arms all night was enough to keep her going for weeks.

"Grab something to drink," Josie said, motioning to the kitchen. "I'm going to get the music going and mingle with the people. I'll be back in a bit."

Logan nodded to her, but once she was out of earshot, turned to Carter. "What do you say we have our own after-party?" she asked.

"I like the way you think," Carter said. She followed her up the stairs, her heart threatening to beat out of her chest.

In the guest room, Logan tossed her overnight bag by the foot of the bed and locked the door behind them. "It may not be a five-star suite, but I did reserve a room for the night," she said.

"I'd give it five stars already." Carter leaned in and slowly kissed her. As the music started to play downstairs, Logan smiled.

"No distractions this time," she said, loosening Carter's tie and using it to pull her in closer.

Slipping out of her jacket, Carter nodded. "Just me and you this time."

"Remember your basketball analogy to having sex?" Logan asked, smiling as she kissed Carter harder this time, her breathing getting more frantic with each touch.

"Yeah, what about it?"

"I guess this is the fourth quarter," Logan said, biting her lip and looking Carter up and down.

"No, baby," Carter said, wrapping her arms tighter around Logan. "This is just the warm-up."

Bella Books, Inc.

Women. Books. Even Better Together.

P.O. Box 10543
Tallahassee, FL 32302

Phone: 800-729-4992
www.bellabooks.com